ELEVEN ELEVEN

ELEVEN
ELEVEN

PAUL
DOWSWELL

BLOOMSBURY
LONDON NEW DELHI NEW YORK SYDNEY

Bloomsbury Publishing, London, New Delhi, New York and Sydney

First published in Great Britain in October 2012 by Bloomsbury Publishing Plc
50 Bedford Square, London, WC1B 3DP

A CIP catalogue record for this book is available from the British Library

ISBN 978 1 4088 2623 2

Typeset by Hewer Text UK Ltd, Edinburgh
Printed in Great Britain by CPI Group (UK) Ltd, Croydon CR0 4YY

1 3 5 7 9 10 8 6 4 2

www.bloomsbury.com

To Grandad Jack and Grandad George,
who survived the Great War and ensured my existence.

Also to J & J and DLD.

CHAPTER 1

Tuesday, 11 November 1918, 2.00 a.m.
Close to the German front line

Axel Meyer was sleeping, his head resting on a black woollen scarf pressed against the train window. Lulled by the steady rhythm of the wheels on the rails, he had managed to fall into his deepest sleep for days, after a nightmare journey from Berlin. Soldiers had been waving red flags and when there were officers around they would whisper, 'Out with the lights, out with the knives.' He nearly saw a man shot in Hannover when an officer had pulled a pistol to restore order. He expected at least an arrest, but the man just melted back into the crowd of soldiers, and the officer must have felt it unwise to try.

Axel struggled to understand why this kind of behaviour was being tolerated by the greatest army on earth. He had never imagined he would fight in the war, but now the High Command had lowered the combat age to sixteen he had been able to enlist in the Imperial German Army.

Axel was bewildered by what he saw. He knew there was so little food at home that people were suffering from slow starvation, but Germany was winning, wasn't she? Hadn't the Russians been beaten? Hadn't vast swathes of territory in the east been given over to Germany? Hadn't Germany's submarines been sinking enemy cargo ships by the score? He felt a rising anger against these traitors with their red flags, these revolutionaries they called *Bolsheviki*.

He'd heard many of them were soldiers who had recently returned from the Eastern Front. Some had even been prisoners of war. They had been infected with communism, the dangerous ideology of the regime that now controlled Russia. These *Bolsheviki* carried the threat of anarchy – a word he had recently learned at school – burning, rape, murder. It was against everything a loyal soldier was supposed to do. He wasn't going to be like that. He was going to make his family – what was left of them – proud of him.

Hearing the men around him talk, he sensed the train was full of these traitors. So he kept his head down and tried not to catch anyone's eye. Especially after that old man in his platoon had picked on him before they'd even left Berlin. 'They're sending *kinder* out now. Look at him.' He pointed to Axel. 'He's barely out of short trousers. You should go home to your mother, lad.'

Axel thought to tell him his mother was dead, but he decided not to reply. He could smell the alcohol on the man's breath and didn't want to antagonise him, especially in the cramped confines of a railway compartment, where he couldn't get away.

After that, Axel tried to make himself inconspicuous. He wondered why the man had singled him out. He wasn't the only sixteen-year-old in that carriage. The man must know this had been decided by the High Command.

Now here he was, heading for the Front, afraid of his own comrades. He told himself to stop worrying about them. It was the enemy he was supposed to be frightened of. Axel had heard all sorts of things about the Tommies and the Yanks. That was who they were up against in this sector. He knew he didn't want to be taken prisoner by either. He had read in the papers that the British dropped hand grenades into the pockets of German soldiers foolish or cowardly enough to surrender. He wasn't going to let anyone capture him.

As his head lolled against the carriage window, he dreamed of *schnitzels* with fried eggs on top, and potatoes coated in butter. Even in his sleep Axel was permanently hungry. He had hoped he'd get better food in the army, but the boys he'd trained with were just as hungry as the villagers back home in Wansdorf.

Axel was jolted from his sleep by a great explosion. It swept over the train, rocking his carriage, followed a second later by the sound of shattering glass. Outside, night became day, and the countryside was flooded with a garish glow which slowly faded to a dull yellow. The man opposite him was screaming and clutching at his throat. A fountain of blood gushed from his neck. Everyone instinctively recoiled. A quick glance at a hole in the fractured window told what had happened. The train had been hit by debris from the explosion. 'Brace yourself for more,' said one of the other men, hurriedly placing his steel helmet on his head.

Another explosion followed, smaller than the first but still enough to shake the carriage like a hurricane gust of wind. Then they heard small-arms fire – spitting like firecrackers.

In a carriage near to theirs there was a sickening thud. Something heavy had fallen out of the sky. The train ground to a screeching halt.

A steady rattling, like heavy rain, began to fall on the carriage roof. Fragments from the explosion. Some penetrated the thin metal but their force was largely spent.

There was more screaming. For a moment Axel was

gripped by a terrible urge to flee through the shattered window. What if the train caught fire? The thought of being burned alive brought a blind panic to his chest. But he breathed deeply and told himself to wait for orders. Besides, there were so many people in the train carriage it would have been impossible to move.

'Are we being attacked?' shouted one of the soldiers in the carriage. 'Let's get out . . .'

An older man – Axel thought he looked old enough to be someone's grandfather – listened for a second then the tension drained from his face. 'That doesn't sound like any fire fight I've been in. I think they've hit an ammunition dump.'

The injured man was being attended to by a soldier sitting next to him, who was covered in blood too now. He had managed to apply a field dressing, but the wounded man's ghastly, chalk-white complexion and vacant eyes suggested he did not have long to live. Axel had seen dead people before – but he had never seen a man die.

'Disembark!' someone shouted, followed by a piercing whistle.

Everyone grabbed packs and rifles and helmets and began to scramble for the exits. Axel felt he was being spat out of the carriage, disgorged in a tide of grey uniforms, with this ragtag collection of young boys and older men. A *Feldwebel* – sergeant – was walking up and down, trying to create order from chaos. Axel stumbled to the rail side, grateful to have escaped, especially when he saw what had hit the carriage behind them. A great steel axle, with a heavy wheel still attached, lay half in and half out of a compartment. Above the pandemonium of the disembarking men he could still hear the cries of those trapped inside.

The train had come to a halt between stations. Axel could see a terrific blaze further down the line and the outline of a town beyond the flames. He could also see star shells floating down to the west, and guessed that was where the Front was. Maybe an hour or so's march away. He felt a stab of fear, but pushed it aside when a boy his own age came over. Like Axel he was wearing a uniform that was too big for his skinny frame. Like Axel his blond hair was cropped short, a style that accentuated his pinched features.

'What's happened?' he asked.

'Something blew up.' Axel shrugged, trying to sound nonchalant. 'Now we have to walk.' Hearing his own voice slightly surprised him. He had spoken to no one for the entire journey.

'You're a Berliner?' said the other boy. 'I know that accent!'

Axel smiled. 'No. But I live close by – in Wansdorf. It's a few kilometres to the west. My parents come from Berlin. And you?'

'Kreuzberg.'

Axel nodded. He had often visited family in that part of Berlin when he was younger.

'It's a madhouse there,' said the boy. 'Red flags. Soldiers' councils. They're turning into Russians – they're even calling for a Soviet Republic.'

'And what d'you think of that?' said Axel warily.

'I don't know,' said the boy. Axel didn't know whether he was being honest or whether he'd decided it was not wise to talk to him about the *Bolsheviki*.

An awkward silence hung between them until the boy fetched an oatmeal biscuit from his pocket and offered it to Axel. 'I'm Erich Becker,' he said, and put out a hand to shake. 'My *Mutti* made these.'

'Thank you,' said Axel, and ate the biscuit at once. He had eaten nothing since breakfast the previous morning. 'As soon as we get to Tommy, we can have our fill of his bully beef, *ja*?'

Axel had heard the British soldiers were well supplied with foods that had become scarce in Germany, especially meat. And he really liked the idea of finding some British chocolate bars as well. Cadbury, Rowntree, Fry – those

7

were the names to look out for. The navy blockade the British had mounted around the coastline had put a stop to any luxuries reaching Germany. Now everyone had to make do with turnips and acorn coffee.

Axel had decided it was his duty to encourage his fellow soldiers – even boys his own age like Erich: keep their spirits up so they would have the courage to fight the enemy. Erich smiled at him but his eyes were dull with fear. Axel hoped his own courage would hold up. His father had sent him off with stern words. *Uphold the good name of the family. Don't bring disgrace on your village. Make your mother proud. She will be watching from heaven.* Axel thought he was a bit old for that now, but he would have loved to believe she was watching over him from somewhere.

A company *Feldwebel* lined them up and they began to march towards the flaming wreckage ahead. The fires were burning bright enough to scorch the skin on their faces. As they marched past, Axel turned to Erich. 'An ammunition truck?'

'A lucky shell, maybe,' he replied. 'Or maybe a Tommy or a Yank flyer dropped a bomb.'

The scene around them was like an image of hell. Whatever had blown up here had set rolling stock alight and ignited several piles of ammunition and shells. Axel wondered if they had all gone off, or whether there was more to come. A few wounded men were being attended to, but most of the casualties were dead – burned to a crisp shell or mutilated beyond recognition. Axel stared straight in front. As they marched towards the town, he wondered what else lay ahead.

CHAPTER 2

2.00 a.m.
Close to the British front line

William Franklin could sense the earth tremble beneath his feet. It wasn't the irregular tremors of an artillery bombardment, or the solid rhythmic stomp of a long column of marching men. This was a deep, heavy rumble – the sort that only a large armoured vehicle would make.

Will felt himself surfacing, like a diver coming up from dark depths. He was so tired he just wanted to stay down in his underwater world for ever. The nearer he came to consciousness, the more he became aware of the soggy cold of that November early morning. It had been raining all of the previous day and his thick trench coat and woollen tunic had soaked up the moisture from the soil.

The men had searched for three hours for a barn or farmhouse to rest in, but every one they had come to had been bursting with other British soldiers. After four years stuck in the trenches, Will's 'King's Own' Royal Lancaster Regiment was on the move.

His platoon had been marching all day and were close to exhaustion. Sometime after midnight their commander, Lieutenant Richardson, decided the roadside would have to do. There was a raised parapet of earth either side, which offered slightly better protection than sleeping out in the open. Will had fallen asleep almost as soon as he unbuckled his pack and laid down his rifle. Now his brief rest was being disturbed.

Will could hear a grinding, clanking sound – so loud he could feel its vibration in his chest. He saw the lieutenant running down the road towards the vehicle, shouting and waving his arms. Will was sorry to see it was him. Richardson had taken the first watch, as he usually did, so that meant they had been asleep for less than an hour.

In the gloom he could make out the silhouette of a single British armoured tractor with caterpillar tracks, pulling a large artillery piece – a heavy howitzer, by what little he could see of it. Will and two of the other boys in his platoon had watched one of them in action the other day – until the artillery commander told them to clear off.

The engine cut abruptly and Lieutenant Richardson's angry voice carried clearly through the night air.

'There's a platoon of men by the side of the road. What made you think it was safe to drive this vehicle down here without checking what was in front of you?'

'Sorry, sir,' said a gruff voice. 'Been ordered to take this up the line, sir, under cover of darkness, sir.'

Will recognised the insolence in the driver's voice. Richardson was barely eighteen – the age Will himself was pretending to be – and had barely started shaving. Richardson was making a good job of being a lieutenant, but beneath the uniform and the officer's bearing and authority, he was still a schoolboy. Will knew his sort from the Officers' Training Corps parades back at home. Will liked him though.

The smell of burning tobacco wafted down the road and caught in his nose. The driver must have a snout on the go. The others in Will's platoon had been disturbed too and some of them were sitting up and instinctively reaching for their Players or Woodbines. Lighter flames and the brief flare of matches lit up faces etched with dirt and exhaustion.

'Settle yourselves, men,' said Richardson. 'We just have to let this half-track past. Then you can get back to sleep.'

The platoon shuffled up the side of the road. Will hated to move. Even in the coldest, dampest spots, if you stayed still, your body heat lent a grudging warmth to the earth and your damp clothes. But if you stirred, the cold bit like shards of broken glass.

The half-track edged forward, close enough now for Will to taste the exhaust in the back of his throat. As it passed, he felt the warmth from the engine on his nose and cheeks. The meagre heat stirred a mad impulse in him. As the caterpillar tracks clanked past, mere inches from his feet, he realised how easy it would be to stretch out a foot and give himself a 'Blighty injury'. That's what the men called the wounds that got you sent back to Blighty – Britain. He stretched his foot out, right to the rim of the metal track.

It was worth it, surely. Will's mind was racing now. Just do it. A crushed foot would have him stretchered to the rear and on a boat back to England. He'd be home within a week. A warm hospital ward. Three hot meals a day. He could sleep as much as he liked. And he would live to see the end of the war. The tractor passed and now the howitzer lumbered after it, its broad armour-plated wheels churning up the muddy road.

Will looked at those wheels with trepidation. It would hurt like hell, and he'd walk with a crutch for the rest of his life. Then he felt a hand on his shoulder. 'Watch that foot there, lad,' whispered Weale, one of the older men in the platoon.

The huge gun slipped in the mud, and the wheel lurched closer to the resting men. Weale pulled Will back just as he hurriedly drew his legs up. The metal plates left deep imprints in the ground right next to him. The driver gunned his engine, trying to gain traction in the soft ground, and then the steady chug of the tractor faded into the distance.

'Lucky escape there, lad,' whispered Weale in his ear. 'Double lucky. If you had caught your leg, they might have thought it deliberate. Boys have been shot fer less.

'Not that I thought that's what you were doing of course,' Weale said with a wink. He patted Will on the back and went back to join his friend Moorhouse. Will's heart was racing, but he knew Weale wouldn't say anything. He liked those two. They'd both been out in France since 1914. If they could survive four years of it, maybe he could too.

Jim Franklin was looking for a man to relieve Richardson for the next hour. Will turned his back on his brother and prayed he wouldn't pick him. Cold and wet as he was, Will was wretchedly weary and desperately needed to rest. The platoon sergeant was careful not to give any of his men the slightest reason to suspect his younger brother had an easier time than the rest of them. Will was also keenly aware that Jim was still angry with him for coming out here in the first place. His mother and father had already lost a son to this war, and Will was only sixteen.

'Battersby, you first, then Uttley,' said Jim. 'Uttley, you can come and get me at oh five hundred.'

Will was safe. At least for the next three hours. He wrapped his trench coat tight around his body and tried to settle. The rain was holding off for now and he began to drift in and out of sleep. Far above he could hear a persistent hum. It sounded like an insect – but it could only be a distant aeroplane. He wondered how the pilots ever managed to find their way back to base on a dark night.

He glanced over to see his brother a few feet away giving instructions to the night watch. Since coming out to France Jim had grown a carapace of steel along with a great bristly moustache. Will understood well why his brother had had to change. How else did you keep a soldier out in no-man's-land in a forward observation post in the middle of the night, with his head and shoulders above the parapet, where he could catch a stray bullet or be snatched by an enemy patrol at any moment? The men in Jim's squad had to be more frightened of their sergeant than they were of the enemy.

Shortly after Will had arrived in C Company, some-one had raided the hamper in the Regimental Aid Post. All the comforts for wounded men – the brandy, the cocoa, the Oxo, even the biscuits – had been taken. Jim had called his platoon to order and told them that unless the goods were returned in the next hour, the whole lot of them would be on night patrol, every night, until they were. It worked.

Another time Will had seen Jim screaming in the face of a young lad who had completely lost his bottle. He was cowering in a trench and crying hysterically, just before they were meant to go over the top. Jim had got him out with the rest of them when the whistle blew. The boy was caught by a machine gun a couple of minutes later.

'He had to go with us. Redcaps would have done for him if he'd stayed in the trench,' Jim told Will afterwards, when they were alone. During an attack, the Military Police combed the start lines just after Z-Hour. And all the troops had been made aware that any man who stayed behind would be shot on the spot.

Now Will's stomach was rumbling and he began to wish he smoked. The others said it stopped you feeling hungry, but whenever he tried a cigarette he coughed his lungs out and the others would laugh and thump him on the back a bit too enthusiastically.

Will liked to stick with the older soldiers when he could. He felt safer with them and enjoyed their banter. He picked their slang up quick enough. 'Cushy' for easy, 'char' for tea – words they had brought back from colonial service in India. There was the newly minted slang from France too, like 'boko' for a lot, a comic pronunciation of *beaucoup*, and 'San Fairy Anne' – it doesn't matter – from *Ça ne fait rien*. But he liked the English slang words the best – like 'gasper' for cigarette, and 'bung' for the tasteless cheese they had in their iron rations, because it was said to 'bung you up'.

But he could sense their sneers when he used those words – he was trying too hard. And he was Sergeant Franklin's brother. They were all right with Will, but he was never really going to be one of them.

He tried to sleep, but he could only doze. He knew they were somewhere near the town of Mons – the place where the British had fought with the German army in the first days of the war. It had taken them over four years to get back here. Four whole years.

In the four months he had been on the Western Front Will had advanced far enough through France and into Belgium to notice how the buildings had changed. Even in the shattered villages he could tell that the houses were more like pictures he had seen at school of Amsterdam or other Dutch places. He wondered what the buildings in Germany would look like.

The thought of entering Germany gave Will a glimmer of confidence but it didn't take his mind off the fact that they were due to attack the town of Saint-Libert in the morning. First light didn't feel too far away, and Will always felt a sickening pit-of-the-stomach fear when he knew he was going to have to fight. Some of the others said he was 'windy' and that it was stupid to worry about it.

'Yer could get killed sitting at the side of the road having a cuppa,' they said, 'if a shell's got yer name on it.'

Jim had taken him to one side and told him men like that were just bragging. 'Everyone gets frightened before a battle, Will, even me,' he whispered. 'If yer not frightened, yer get careless. Being frightened is good. You make sure you're frightened when we have to fight. You'll stay alive that way.'

After another few minutes the cold overtook Will's tiredness and he sat up. In the sky a parachute flare floated slowly down. It was too far away to cast any light over their own position but close enough to make him realise they could be in the thick of the fighting in less than an hour.

Another kind of noise reached him now. Far to the east he heard the metallic grind of wheels on tracks. He guessed they were troop trains – German reinforcements for their front line. Hearing the distant shunting and creaking brought back sudden memories of home. Sounds of trains in the night while he was tucked up snug in bed. He thought of his room back in Lancaster, in his family's terraced house with its fine Minton tiles. He could almost taste the bread his mother baked every morning, and the comforting smell of the coal-fired range in the kitchen. What he'd give for a slice of that bread with butter and his mum's home-made raspberry jam. His stomach lurched and gurgled.

He tried hard to steer his mind away from food, and thought instead of Alice. He carried a tatty photograph of her in his tunic pocket – wrapped in greaseproof paper to protect it from the damp. He was so familiar with it he did not often get it out to look at. She was staring stiffly into the camera, her face an enigma – neither smiling nor scowling. Will often wondered what she was thinking when that shot was taken.

He could picture her in Lancaster Royal Grammar School's assembly hall, playing at the great black grand piano they had, after most of the boys had gone home. Will had been a pupil there, before all this. He often stayed late to work in the library. Alice was the headmaster's daughter. He would listen to her play, lingering at the hall entrance so she wouldn't notice him. She always stopped the minute she knew he was there.

A great thunderous explosion rent the night air – and a billowing flash lit up the sky. All of the men sat up at once. They reached for their rifles and anxiously scanned the surrounding area. 'What's Fritz up to?' said Battersby.

A series of smaller explosions followed. Like lightning and thunder, they saw the flashes first; then the sound rolled over a few moments later.

Sergeant Franklin loomed out of the dark and told them all to stand down. 'Nothing to worry about. Sounds like an ammunition dump or a supply train,' he said. 'Maybe Fritz got careless with a shell. Or maybe one of our pilot boys dropped a bomb on them.' He gave a little chuckle. 'That'll keep 'em occupied for a while.'

After a while, Will heard the creaking and clanking of trains from the German lines start up again. There were men and boys over there, disembarking on to platforms or sidings. Maybe they were as frightened as he was. He hoped so.

CHAPTER 3

2.00 a.m.
American Air Service airbase

Eddie Hertz slept in a plush feather bed in a farmhouse in Prouvy – close to the Belgian border. His squadron had moved forward from Doullens three weeks ago and he was settling in nicely.

His lodgings suited him well. It was right on the edge of his airbase and close enough for him to hear the empty shell case that hung by the operations room. When the duty officer hit that with an iron bar, they all had to rush over at once. The other flyboys in the American Air Service First Pursuit Group were having to make do with corrugated iron sheds or, even worse, tents, for their accommodation. Eddie had outbid his fellow flyers for the rent on this room. It was worth every franc. This was most definitely not the season for a tent, especially as the ground round here was so boggy.

Eddie had never been this close to the action before, but the war was moving at a rapid pace. The airbase at

21

Doullens, which had been his home since he'd arrived in France in early 1918, was now too far away from the Front.

Despite the comfort of his lodgings, Eddie was having a restless night. His thoughts drifted to Céline – a dark-haired French girl he knew. Thinking about her made a pleasant change from the concerns that usually plagued his resting hours. Céline had been working at a field hospital close to Doullens and she and her fellow nurses were regular guests at the pilots' mess. She'd also been posted forward, close to Eddie's new base. He was sure fate was working in his favour. They talked about a bullet with your name on it. Céline had his name on her. He liked her a lot.

That night Eddie had told her the pilots all thought a scarf from a pretty girl was a sure-fire good-luck charm to keep them safe in the sky. How could she refuse? It was expensive too. Pure silk. She must like him, to give him that.

Now, as Eddie drifted on the edge of sleep, the room was suddenly illuminated by a great flash of light. Then the roar of a terrible explosion tore through the night.

He sat bolt upright, muttering, 'What the hell was that?'

He rushed to the window, but outside was total darkness. He wondered if the Germans were mounting an attack, but dismissed the idea. If Fritz really was going on the offensive, there'd be more explosions. Eddie thought the Germans were a busted flush. There were hardly any Boche planes up these days. They were done. The war was almost over.

Eddie said 'Boche' when he was around Céline, like she said it, to entertain her. That was what the Frenchies called the Germans. But then he would feel like a creep. His family was German. He was only first-generation American himself. He even spoke the language.

He wondered whether or not to get dressed and report to the briefing hut. He pulled on his trousers, then decided not to bother. No one was sounding the alarm, and his bed was more inviting than the cold air of this autumn night. He cursed himself for dithering. His old girlfriend in New York, Janie Holland, she was always changing her mind. This hat or that, this dress or that skirt. It drove him mad. It was a relief when her letter arrived at his airbase telling him she had met a US Navy captain and that was the end of Eddie and Janie. His parents adored her though – and their wealthy families were friends. 'It's good to marry money, Eddie,' said his mother. 'That way you know they're not just marrying you for yours.'

The Hertz fortune was founded on electrical domestic appliances – toasters, kettles, hotplates, ovens – and had netted the Hertzes an apartment overlooking Central Park and the best education for Eddie, and his younger brother, Bobby, that money could buy.

It was only over the last few weeks he'd really fallen for Céline. She never asked him about his family or his money. Maybe he'd ask her to go to Paris with him. He'd been last month. It was beautiful, but unsettling. Full of old men. The only young ones he'd seen had missing limbs or other nasty wounds. And all those women in their widow's black.

He tried to sleep, but it was impossible.

Last night a group of British flyers had joined them in the mess – a return visit from the airbase down in Monchaux-sur-Écaillon, where the American pilots had been invited the week before. It had been a great evening, until the British started singing their macabre songs. One of them went:

> Take the cylinder out of my kidneys
> The connecting rod out of my brain
> From the small of my back take the camshaft
> And assemble the engine again.

The other guys in the squadron roared with laughter, but Eddie could only muster a polite smile. Céline didn't find it funny either and didn't even pretend to be amused. They both agreed the British had a strange sense of humour. Actually the song made Eddie feel a bit queasy. He told himself it was the wine, but he'd sobered up a bit and the song still kept going round and round in his head.

He'd been in France nine months now, and he'd seen enough gruesome accidents to know exactly what happened to a flyer when fate deserted him. Three days ago, at around ten in the morning, he had landed his plane on a flat field behind the Allied lines where he had downed a Fokker triplane – his fourth kill.

As he ran towards the wreckage, he saw a crowd of soldiers, who he took to be British Tommies. They stood in a semicircle by the downed plane, which was still burning around its mangled engine.

The pilot had been thrown clear and the crowd was keeping a respectable distance from his lifeless body. He lay on his back, arms and legs flat on the ground, eyes open. Eddie could see he was a handsome fellow, even though his face was covered in sooty, greasy oil. A shock of dark hair, a strong jaw, not much older than him. They even looked quite alike. But his clothes were badly burned and half hanging off him.

Eddie had seen dead bodies before – some of them

burned to a cinder and others so badly mutilated they were unrecognisable. This death was one he was personally responsible for and it had particularly touched him. The fellow he had shot down and killed could have been his kith and kin. If his parents' families hadn't left Germany for New York forty years before, that dead man could have been his comrade-in-arms. He could have been him.

Eddie had walked towards the body, unsettled by the stillness of death. He knew the man had had a terrible end. He had seen his body jerk forward when Eddie had fired into the plane. That hadn't killed him – that would have been a merciful death. Instead, the fellow had struggled to put out the flames around his engine, beating at them with his gloved hands. The fire went out – more through luck than the efforts of the wounded pilot, Eddie suspected – but the engine had died and the man had made a gallant effort to guide his aircraft down to earth. He nearly made it, but the plane stalled close to the ground and crashed with a great grinding *crump*.

Eddie knelt over the body, unnerved by the man's sightless gaze. He almost expected the eyes to follow him or for the pilot to suddenly cough or breathe.

He reached down and took the man's identification tag from a chain on his neck. That was part of the flyer's code

– pilots took it upon themselves to notify their enemies who had died and who had been captured. They would drop the tags and a wreath on the nearest enemy airbase. Flyers on both sides did it. Then he closed the man's eyes. He was still warm, of course. Ten minutes ago he was as alive as Eddie and all the others standing there gawping. Some of them were thawing themselves by the blazing machine. That annoyed Eddie. It seemed discourteous.

'Hey, get away,' he yelled at the soldiers. 'That thing might go off again. Or the ammunition might ignite.'

'You can piss off, Yank,' came a voice from the other side of the plane, obscured by smoke. The others laughed. Eddie half recognised the accent – they certainly weren't British – probably Australians or New Zealanders.

He had expected them to greet him as a hero. Instead, they looked on him as some sort of curiosity. 'Off yer go, mate,' said another soldier – a barrel of a man with sergeant stripes on his sleeves – and placed a firm hand on Eddie's shoulder. As he turned to leave, the same fellow said, 'Well done, but as yer soar off back into the sky, and then back to yer comfy little bed, spare a thought for the poor bloody infantry.'

Eddie got back into his aircraft and took off, feeling a little foolish. As he banked over the scene, none of the soldiers below paid him any attention. So much for all that 'Knights of the Sky' crap he had read about in the newspapers and magazines back home.

That dead man's face haunted him now as he tried to get back to sleep. Eddie's fourth victim. One more, if he lived that long, and he'd be an Ace. That would make his mother proud. He tried to turn his thoughts back to Céline. Her silk scarf hung over a chair, still with a hint of her perfume. He recognised it. *Quelques Fleurs*. The scent hung in the air like a ghost. Eddie rolled over and pulled the blankets over his head. 'One day, when this is all over, I shall take her back to New York,' he told himself. 'One day I might even ask her to marry me!'

How could she refuse? A rich, handsome American – was there a more eligible man in the whole of France?

As Eddie drifted half a world away, his mother Else Hertz drew back a thick velvet curtain in the grand living room of their Upper East Side apartment so she could look down over Central Park. It was a cloudy night, but for a moment the moon came through and the trees were lit with a silver glow. A lone horse and cart clopped past, seven storeys below, the sound of hooves on asphalt almost drowned by the thrum of motorcars on still-crowded Fifth Avenue.

Walter, her husband, had gone to his room in a huff,

and Bobby, their sixteen-year-old son, had been sent to bed in disgrace. The family had been dining at Delmonico's, and Else and Walter had argued over how much wine Bobby should be allowed to drink. She had been right. One glass would have been quite sufficient for a boy his age. There'd been similar scenes with Eddie only a year or two before.

She reached for a copy of *The New York Times* and looked for a story she had read that morning.

YALE MAN DOWNS FOURTH HUN

Eddie Hertz, the nineteen-year-old heir to the Hertz family fortune, claimed his fourth kill over Flanders on Thursday. Showing the kind of grit that earned him a place on the Yale Bulldogs football team, the American Air Service First Pursuit Group flyer chased a Hun triplane for over an hour before he sent him crashing to the ground.

Else cut the piece from the page and placed it in an envelope addressed to her friend Mary Holland. Things had been a little cool between them since Mary's daughter Janie had dropped Eddie for that sailor. Now Eddie was a war hero! This was the fourth time he'd made the papers this year.

29

She sealed her letter and left it in the tray for the maid. But when Else finally retired to bed an hour later, she felt uneasy. She wished Eddie could be doing nothing on a destroyer in the middle of the north Atlantic, like Janie's new fellow, rather than taking to the skies over Flanders in one of those flying death traps. She looked wistfully at the photograph of her boy in his pilot uniform, taken the day before he boarded the troopship to England. He looked barely more than a child, and she'd give up everything she had just to see him again.

CHAPTER 4

3.00 a.m.

Despite his exhaustion, Will was not going to sleep again that night. He felt restless and couldn't help dwelling on how he had ended up here at the Front, when he could easily have spent another two years at home.

It had been one of those warm spring days in early April and Alice's father, Dr Hayworth, had invited Will out on a family picnic. Dr Hayworth knew he and Alice were sweethearts, but Will was forbidden to visit their house. Maybe, he thought, this invite was a sign that they were coming round to the idea.

They had driven out to the Lune Valley with another car containing Alice's uncle and her cousins, along with their pet parrot. Will had never been in a car before and he felt light-headed with excitement. It seemed against the laws of nature to be able to drive along that fast, without a team of horses. Dr Hayworth took bends at alarming speed, and when he ground the gears and cursed under

31

his breath Will and Alice caught each other's eye and had a fit of the giggles.

After they'd eaten a lunch of cold roast chicken and potato salad, the women and girls of the party sat around on deckchairs chatting. Will was surprised to see they even let Pru the parrot perch on top of her cage. 'Why doesn't she fly away?' he asked Alice.

'She's had her wings clipped, silly!' she said.

Will had hoped he and Alice would be able to go for a riverside walk. Instead, he was approached by Dr Hayworth. 'We need to have a talk, my lad,' he said, and guided him away from the others.

Hayworth came straight to the point. The German spring offensive was making great inroads into the Allied front line. All the gains of the previous three years had been lost, and now even Paris was threatened. 'If you're man enough to court my daughter,' he said, pointedly repeating the words of a recruitment poster Will had seen around town, 'then you're man enough to fight for her honour against the Hun.'

Will protested he was not old enough to join up. But Hayworth told him that that hadn't stopped those two valiant boys Boothby and Solomons. Both had honoured the school with their warrior spirit. Now the war with Russia was over and the Hun had only the Western Front to fight on, the British army would need every soldier they could get.

So Will went along to the recruiting office in Lancaster Town Hall and spent half an hour being measured and filling in forms. He told them he was eighteen. 'Course you are, son,' said the recruiting sergeant with a wink.

Alice's face fell when Will told her. He'd thought she'd be proud of him. She pleaded with him not to do it, but it was too late, he'd already signed the papers. That was when she told him her parents had always chided her for taking a shine to him, a boy whose own father worked in a textile warehouse. Will realised then that Dr Hayworth's real motive was to get him away from Alice.

His father congratulated him for being a brave lad, but his mother said nothing at all, before disappearing into the kitchen to prepare the tea. After he had gone to bed, he heard them arguing. Will wasn't sure what had stopped them going down to the recruiting station and telling them he was too young. He half wished now that they had.

Will's other brother, Stanley, had gone missing at Passchendaele. Will's mum had said not knowing what had happened to him was worse than finding out. So when one of Stanley's mates came home on leave, Will's dad

33

got him drunk down at the Weaver's Arms. The lad told him that Stan had drowned. 'He's not a bloody sailor!' spluttered Will's dad. 'How can you drown in the army?'

It had rained like cats and dogs for weeks before the battle began. Passchendaele was a vast sea of sucking mud. They had gone on a raid in the middle of the night. Stanley had been sucked into the mud and sank. By the time they got to him, he'd gone under. It wasn't the heroic end gallant soldiers dreamed of.

When Will went out, they got Jim to have a word with the commander of his company, to make sure Will would serve alongside his brother. Lillie Franklin was convinced that if he had Jim to look after him he would be safe.

Will was sent to Grantham in Lincolnshire for his basic training. The weeks he spent there passed in a blur, but the answer to a question one of the recruits asked about taking prisoners had stuck in his head: 'Well, lads, every prisoner is another mouth to feed. It's another day's rations. Think about that when you've got some Hun yelling "*Kamerad*" at you.' 'Friend', that meant. That's what they said when they wanted to surrender.

He never resented the constant cleaning and polishing and the bone-weary exhaustion of his training. The whole point of it, he told himself, was to enable him to survive.

The thought of gas terrified him – especially when they had to put on their clumsy 'gaspirators', as the men jokingly called them, and pass through a hut full of the stuff. Will found he could breathe all right, but the mask was hellishly uncomfortable and made his face sweat and itch. And his clothes stank for the next three days.

He paid close attention to the ins and outs of the Lee-Enfield rifle and its firing mechanism, the workings of the Lewis machine gun, the correct use of the Mills hand grenade and, somewhat queasily, 'the offensive spirit of the bayonet'. Fighting at close quarters was what worried him most. The prospect of having to shove a bayonet into another soldier's gut made him feel sick. Bombs, rifles and machine guns all did their work at a distance. With a bayonet you had to get right up close. His instructors were quite plain about where the best places to strike were: the throat, the chest and the groin. The bayonet, they declared, was the best possible weapon for close-quarter combat. If you fired your rifle when fighting hand to hand, you stood every chance of the shot passing straight through your opponent's body and hitting your comrade. Bayonets were the ideal weapon. It didn't take long for Will to realise that his German adversaries were almost certainly being told the same thing.

* * *

In early June they were ready. Until he'd joined the army, Alice and the teachers at his school were the poshest people he'd known. Now, on his last day in Grantham, they were herded into a large hall and given a pep talk by a portly colonel with a bristly moustache who was even posher. He said 'hice' and 'rhum' instead of 'house' and 'room', and Will had some difficulty understanding him. The colonel warned them of the penalties of breaching the 'Army Act'. This would lead to 'trouble', as he put it, and even 'shooting at the hands of your own comrades'. He told them that fear was not a crime, but an inability to control that fear was a contagious disease that needed to be isolated and cured with the utmost severity. Will left the hall feeling terrified, and unwilling to catch the eye of any of his fellow recruits.

Next morning, on a breezy sunny day, they took the ferry across the Channel to Calais and then a short train journey to the huge training camp at Étaples. Here, the new arrivals were billeted right next to a Casualty Clearing Station while they awaited their first taste of the front line. This temporary hospital was a vast camp – taking up maybe half a square mile of tents and wooden huts.

They were immediately put to work stretchering the wounded off the trains that came in twice a day. The gas casualties were the worst. Gasping for breath, coughing up bloody lumps, their uniforms still stinking of the gas that had got them. Carrying the shell-blast victims was a nightmare too. They screamed every time they were moved, as shattered bones grated together. Right next door to the Casualty Clearing Station was a vast cemetery – thousands and thousands of graves. It might have been practical, but it was hardly a reassuring sight.

When he got to the Front and told Jim about the Clearing Station cemetery, his brother waved him away in scorn. 'Toughen up, sunshine,' he had said. 'That's nothing. When we came up through the reserve trenches for the big push at the Somme, they marched us past two open graves, great big ones, dug that morning for what was to come. I yelled out "Eyes left" to stop the men seeing them, but I don't think I fooled anyone.'

Now, as Will lay on the same cold, dark earth, he tried not to think about those burial pits, and all the men whose bodies had been placed in them. He had been three months now at the Front. Every minute, every hour, was a battle against the bullet, shell or bayonet that fate had written his name on.

CHAPTER 5

3.00 a.m.

Axel Meyer was relieved to be marching away from the blazing wreckage. Amid the charred wood and burning oil there was a horrible smell that he did not recognise. It was sweet and putrid and a little like roast pork or beef. With a jolt he realised that it must be burning bodies.

'Where d'you think we're going?' he asked his new friend.

'I don't know,' Erich replied. 'I imagine to some sort of barracks, or at least somewhere where we can get something to eat.'

'Silence in the ranks!' shouted the *Feldwebel* who was escorting them forward – a stern-looking man of around thirty, who towered over most of the soldiers here. They had already seen him kicking and punching some of the men. He came down the line and grabbed Erich hard by the arm. 'If I have to tell you two again, it'll be *Anbinden* for the both of you.'

'What the hell is *Anbinden?*' whispered Axel when the *Feldwebel* went back to the head of the line.

Erich rubbed his arm. It felt as if it had been in a vice. 'They tie you to a tree or a post or something like that,' he said, 'and leave you for several hours where you might get hit by enemy fire.'

Axel shuddered.

He hoped Erich was right about the barracks. He hadn't had a bath or a shower for several days now, and he felt seedy. Everyone smelled of sweat and mothballed *feldgraue* – field-grey – uniforms and boot polish, so he wasn't bothered about that. He just thought having a decent wash would perk him up a bit. At the moment he was so tired he felt as if he was wading through porridge. He thought, with a desperate longing, of his feather bed back in Wansdorf.

There was some muttering up front, strange noises. Suddenly the *Feldwebel* called the column to a halt and hauled a soldier from the ranks. He flung him to the ground and pointed a pistol at him. 'You have one final opportunity to prove your worth to the Fatherland,' he said. 'If I hear you, or any of the rest of you, bleating, I will shoot you without hesitation.' He dragged the terrified soldier back to his feet, then kicked him hard in the backside towards the column. They started marching again.

'What happened?' asked Erich under his breath.

'I heard them doing it on the train,' whispered Axel. 'Some of the soldiers bleat like sheep to slaughter, to mock the officers. They heard the French soldiers did it, earlier in the war. I reckon he was trying to start it off.'

The column took a sharp turn to the left and Axel prayed they would be resting soon. As they marched to the west he noticed a succession of bright lights floating down in the sky. These must be parachute flares. Both sides regularly launched them to deter night attacks.

Soon afterwards Axel heard the distinctive rattle of a machine gun. He had been exposed to that sound plenty of times in his training camp, but now, for the first time, that *rat-tat-tat-tat* was live ammunition being fired at another human being, caught in the glow of the flare. All at once he realised with a rising dread what it would mean to be hit by a machine gun. They had told him in training that these weapons fired six hundred rounds a minute. Ten bullets a second. He and the other cadets all cooed in wonder – what a fantastic device! But here, so close to the Front, ten bullets a second took on a more sinister meaning when it was your body they were aiming at.

In the light from the flares they could make out a church spire ahead, and the roofs and chimneys of a small town. In a couple of minutes they had marched into the central square, where they could see groups of other German soldiers sitting or lying on the ground. They looked exhausted, and many of them were asleep. The stench of unwashed muddy clothes rose off them. It reminded Axel of his dog, Falken, after he'd been for a dip in a particularly fetid pool of water. When he was doing his training, he'd heard all sorts of nicknames for a front-line soldier: *Dreckfresser* – mud eater, *Frontschweine* – front swine. He'd liked the more humorous nicknames better, like *Hans Wurst* – Hans Sausage. But these men were definitely *Frontschweine*. Just as surely as he would be if he survived his first taste of combat.

Over on the far side of the square, there were a few field guns and piles of munitions. The town was barely more than a big village and, as far as Axel could tell in the dark, it seemed almost undamaged by the war.

'Stand easy!' shouted the *Feldwebel*, and the soldiers took off their heavy packs and laid down their rifles. They sat on the cobbled square, leaning on their packs or against one another's backs.

Axel was exhausted. He wondered what he could throw away to lighten his pack. His father had given him a pamphlet *Kraftsprüche aus der Heiligen Schrift für die Kriegszeit* – 'Helpful passages from the Holy Scriptures in Wartime' – that seemed to be a good candidate. Since his earnest prayers to keep his family safe had fallen on deaf ears he had not felt the same about God. But Axel hesitated. He rifled through the pages and put the pamphlet back in his pocket. Where he was going he needed all the help he could get.

There was a field kitchen set up close by and Axel could smell something cooking – soup probably. An older soldier came round and told them to queue for their ration.

The *Gulaschkanone* – stew gun – sat smoking away in the corner. They called it that because its tall stove chimney could be lowered flat when the kitchen had to be moved. That made it look a bit like a cannon. Axel thought it had been misnamed. He'd give anything for some real stew – a nice thick beef-and-dumpling with peas and carrots and potatoes. What they usually got from the *Gulaschkanone* was some sort of thin vegetable soup – and you needed to be pretty clever to tell what sort of vegetables were in it. They had their soup with black *Kriegsbrot* – war bread – which was bulked out with wood shavings. That wasn't a rumour. You could see them in the slices.

When he got to the front of the queue and was given a hunk of black bread and a ladle full of grey-green soup, he asked, 'Where are we? Do you know what's happening?'

The cook leaned closer and whispered, 'This place is called Saint-Libert. I think they're sending that lot back east –' he nodded to the exhausted men on the other side of the square – 'and you are going forward.'

So, they were going straight to the Front. Axel nodded. His mouth was too dry to speak. He didn't feel ready to face men who had been fighting for months already, maybe years.

He sat down with Erich and they both devoured their soup, wiping their mess tins clean with the bread. It tasted of nothing they could recognise – in fact it was more of a texture than an actual flavour – like wallpaper paste. But it was hot and it filled a hole. When they had finished, Axel whispered, 'We're going into action. I thought we'd have a rest first. I didn't think we'd be sent straight to the Front.'

'Form up,' shouted the *Feldwebel*.

Axel and Erich placed themselves at the very rear of the column this time – as far away as possible from the *Feldwebel*. It felt safer, being at the back.

As they marched past the railway station at the far end of the square, Axel could see silhouettes of men on the roof. They were holding wires and small packages. 'What are they doing?' he whispered to Erich.

An older man in front of them leaned round and

said, 'It looks like they're wiring up the railway station. Ready to blow it up. They've probably put explosives on the rails too. When we go, they will destroy the town. Leave them nothing that's useful.'

Axel wondered if he would pass this way again. He looked at the eastern sky. It was still dark, with no glimmer of the approaching dawn. While it was dark, he felt safe.

But, as if to prove him wrong, he heard a distant whistle. 'Incoming shell,' whispered the man in front. There was a dull explosion further to the north.

'Not here at least,' said Erich.

But there were more, coming in at steady intervals, getting closer. Axel heard a whistling sound growing louder by the second. He wanted to quicken his pace, or start to run, but he was too frightened of the *Feldwebel* to break rank.

There was a *crack* and a shattering sound in the square behind him, like someone hitting bricks and mortar with a large lump hammer. Axel expected a crushing explosion, but there was nothing more. He glanced behind, but it was too dark to see.

The parachute flares still lit up the sky, and as they grew closer to the Front, Axel began to imagine their distant glow was reflecting on his jacket buttons. One old soldier had told him to rub mud on them, but he hadn't dared besmirch his uniform like that.

The intermittent rattle of machine guns was growing louder.

As the column marched out of the town, resentful eyes observed their departure from an attic room of Café Remy, on the edge of the town. Georges de Winne, the owner of the establishment, peered down the barrel of his stolen Mauser rifle and drew a bead on the last head in the column. It was too dark to see properly but it made no difference. He pulled the trigger and the firing pin clicked in an empty chamber. He didn't really know why he did it, but it made him feel better.

De Winne scratched his great black moustache and sat down with a sigh. One of these days, he told himself, he would have the courage to kill some of these Boche. Right now, he had no ammunition for his gun, and he was too frightened to ask for some from the few people he knew in Saint-Libert who formed part of the town's shady resistance. He hoped they had forgotten he had offered to keep the gun for them. Its presence in his house, tucked out of sight in a pile of old newspapers and carpets in the attic, caused him constant anxiety. When the Boche had arrived, midway through their triumphant

45

march through Belgium in the far-off summer of 1914, they had been ruthless with any Belgian civilians caught with firearms. There had been summary executions. Sometimes women and children were shot too. The executions provoked a great deal of impotent rage, but they had ensured minimum resistance and even a measure of surly cooperation.

When de Winne thought about all the things he had had to do for the Germans, who had made frequent use of his bar, resentment simmered in his gut like sour wine. This was the fifth autumn the Boche had been there in Saint-Libert, but, he had to admit to himself, he had done quite well out of the occupation. Georges de Winne knew people. He could be relied on by the Germans to find a duck or a suckling pig for a regimental commander planning a celebratory feast, and in return the Germans had ensured the de Winne family had more than their fair share of provisions. It was a difficult state of affairs. While the other townspeople grew increasingly wan from their near-starvation rations, he and his wife and children were obviously well fed still. Of course people began to talk, and de Winne couldn't help but notice the stares. He felt guilty about that too. So he started to hoard his extra provisions – the attic was full of tins of beans and cans of stewed beef. His family didn't starve, but at least they didn't look as plump as they used to.

The Germans kept a tight grip on news in Saint-Libert but even the dullest plough hand could tell that the balance of power was shifting. The soldiers that passed through the town on the way to fight the Allies looked increasingly old or young. The ones coming back east came through in greater numbers, and many of them were wounded. For the last couple of weeks, when the wind was in the right direction, it was possible to hear the sound of shell fire. Over the last few days de Winne had even heard the rattle of machine guns, and one or two shells had fallen on the town. He worried about his house, of course, they all did, but the days of fear and kowtowing and endless petty restrictions stipulated by notices put up around town *Auf Befehl des Stadtkommandanten* – by order of the commander – were drawing to a close.

CHAPTER 6

Private train of Marshal Foch
Compiègne forest, north of Paris, 4.00 a.m.

One hundred kilometres behind the front line, Captain George Atherley surveyed the scene before him and fought back a deep desire to yawn. The pall of tobacco smoke that hung over the railway carriage was making his eyes water and he was desperate for a cigarette himself. He needed something to keep him awake. He knew this was history in the making, and he was lucky to be here taking notes and witnessing it.

The German delegation had been escorted across the duckboards on to Marshal Foch's private train at two o'clock; now it was four o'clock and they were still talking. It was cold in the carriage, and although the paraffin heaters were taking the chill off, they added to the drowsy atmosphere.

The Germans had been pushing for talks since early October, but negotiations had only been going on in earnest for three days. Every hour, every minute, brought more needless deaths. The German delegation had been arguing every point, but the British and French were giving nothing away. Why should they, thought Atherley. Germany was on the point of collapse. Berlin, Munich, perhaps half the country, was about to fall into anarchy. Just like the Russians with their Bolsheviks the year before.

Atherley was there to take the minutes on behalf of the British government, represented here by the First Sea Lord. Sir Rosslyn Wemyss was as forbidding and stuffy as his name and rank suggested, but he wasn't as cold-hearted as Foch. Foch was merciless. The Boche had asked for it though, thought Atherley. They had started the war.

But, just tonight, he had actually begun to feel sorry for the Germans. Matthias Erzberger, the man they had sent to represent the shaky coalition that held power in Berlin now the Kaiser had abdicated, was a nobody, raised to prominence, and no doubt future infamy, for this catastrophic peace treaty they were about to sign. Him and Count Alfred von Obersdorff sitting next to him – a somebody from the Foreign Ministry. They would be blamed for this. The army had sent a major general, sitting there in his ridiculous *Pickelhaube* helmet and overcoat, looking like a cartoon Hun. Nobody above a division commander was willing to represent the army.

49

There were no generals, no field marshals. The Imperial German Navy had only sent a humble captain. A fellow called Vanselow.

The victors, on the other hand, were there in all their glory. The French had Marshal Foch, Supreme Commander of the Allied Armies, looking unforgiving with his great walrus moustache and the killer eyes of a cat with a bird in its mouth. The British had their First Sea Lord. Atherley was in the army, but he was happy to admit it was only proper that the Senior Service represent the Empire at this hour. The Yanks weren't there. Atherley didn't really understand why that was.

Now they were arguing about terms again. The French were demanding the Germans hand over 2,000 aircraft. How could they, pleaded Erzberger, after hurried consultation with his military colleagues, when they had only 1,700 left?

They hammered it out. The figures were astounding. The Allies were asking for 5,000 artillery pieces, 30,000 machine guns, 5,000 locomotives – Atherley scribbled it all down – 150,000 railway carriages; he had to interrupt to ask for that figure again. Wemyss looked daggers at him . . . and the entire submarine fleet.

The Germans held out for more concessions. There were women and children starving at home. Would the blockade be lifted immediately? Every day civilians were dying for want of nourishment. The longer they went on arguing, the more would die.

Yes, and more of our soldiers and yours, thought Atherley. He wasn't really concerned about the German civilians, although a little part of him had to concede he could hardly blame the women and children for starting the war.

All right, agreed Foch and Wemyss. The Allies 'would contemplate the provisioning of Germany during the Armistice as shall be found necessary'.

Contemplate. As he wrote it down, Atherley gave a little smirk at the mealy-mouthed wording of that particular concession.

Then that was it. They had finished. Papers were to be signed. Atherley looked at his watch. It was 5.10. The war was over. History had been made. The mincing machine would grind to a halt. They all agreed to say they had signed at 5.00, and then the required six hours to bring the Armistice into effect would end the war at eleven o'clock, Paris time. That had a nice ring to it, they thought. The eleventh hour of the eleventh day of the eleventh month.

Atherley felt a little indignant. Surely they could bring it to a halt quicker than that? He had a younger brother out near Mons, and he'd lost two already. Both of them on the Somme in 1916. He hoped Lieutenant Peter Atherley, of the Surrey Rifles, would have the good sense to keep his head down. Some would have to die in the last morning of the war – probably a hell of a lot of men, especially with the American divisions. Their staff officers had reputations to seal, and if they were anything like the British staff officers he'd served with, they wouldn't be too fussy about the cost.

Erzberger was speaking again. He seemed like a man at the end of his tether. 'The German people will preserve their liberty and unity, despite every kind of violence. A nation of seventy million people suffers but it does not die.'

Foch looked at him with plain disinterest. '*Très bien*,' he said.

The Germans left with a reminder that the Armistice would hold for thirty days, to be renewed once a month thereafter. Hostilities would begin within forty-eight hours if any of the terms were breached. There were no handshakes.

The war had six hours left to run.

CHAPTER 7

4.00 a.m.

Axel's combat group marched away from the town. As far as he could tell by the flares, and occasional rattle of gunfire, they were going parallel to the Front, heading south or maybe south-west. Axel hated not knowing where he was or the names of the places they were passing through. It made him feel as if he had no control over what was happening. No control over his life. Maybe it was the damp night air, but now, as they approached the front line, Axel sensed a distinct lack of fighting spirit among his fellow recruits.

The *Feldwebel* called a halt and counted off half the men to join a unit already dug in at the side of the road they were marching along. He grabbed them by the arm and pushed them away from the remaining soldiers. There was certainly no encouraging pat on the back for anyone. For the soldier who had been flung to the ground and threatened with execution, there was a sharp cuff on the back of the head. 'Watch this one,' said the *Feldwebel* to one of the position commanders. 'He doesn't deserve a second chance.'

The rest of them marched on, the *Feldwebel* leading the way. Axel cursed himself for positioning himself at the back. He was desperate to take off his heavy pack and collapse on the ground. And his boots were a poor fit. He could feel a raw blister developing on one heel. They leaked too. One foot was sodden, the other merely clammy. He wished he had a change of socks. Having wet feet made you feel wet all over.

But he tried to cheer up – he didn't want to appear weak in front of Erich. It was good the new soldiers were being split up. They could fight with experienced men rather than as a bunch of frightened first-timers.

They arrived in a small village. From what Axel could see in the dark it was little more than a medieval church with a tower, and a few farm buildings and humble cottages, set around a manor house that had seen better days. Shutters hung loose at the windows, and tiles were missing from the roof.

The *Feldwebel* ordered the men to break ranks. 'There's the barn. Sleep in the straw. You must be ready to hold this village when it gets light.'

Axel was dead on his feet. As the men took their packs from their backs, a distant whistle caught their attention. It was rapidly growing closer. 'Take cover!' shouted the *Feldwebel* as shells screamed down around them.

Great fountains of earth exploded from the ground, then came the stench of cordite, which Axel could taste at the back of his throat.

'Did they see us in those parachute flares?' said Erich. His voice seemed far away and he was staring straight ahead – detached, almost on the edge of panic.

'Quiet,' said Axel brusquely. 'There may be more to come.'

Erich snapped out of his stupor and looked at him angrily. 'So what are we going to do? Listen for the shells coming in and dodge out of the way?'

Axel put a hand on his friend's shoulder. 'I'm sorry.'

A few of the squad staggered uneasily to their feet. 'Keep down,' snapped the *Feldwebel*.

They waited, with the smell of wet earth all around them, barely daring to breathe. At any moment any of them could be ripped to pieces, or horribly wounded and having to face a lingering death. That was what Axel feared the most. A shot through the head, you wouldn't know what had hit you. But something that ripped your bowels out or left you missing both legs . . . that was what had kept him awake at night. He had seen plenty of casualties back at home over the last four years.

There was Werner, a few years ahead of him in school, who had lost an arm and a leg to shell fire early in the war. Now his mother pushed him around in a wheelchair. They had taken him to watch a school football match, but had left early when he became agitated. Werner had been a keen footballer.

Later, in 1916, the Meyers heard that Axel's older brother, Otto, had been killed at Verdun. Axel had been shocked by the brutal utility of the *Kriegsministerium* postcard that arrived to notify the family of their loss. A simple stamp on plain white paper '*Gefallen für's Vaterland*' – Fallen for the Fatherland – and a scribbled name.

Axel had gone to church that Sunday with his family and Otto's fiancée, Rosa, and special prayers had been said for his brother. They walked back home in silence to find an army motorbike messenger waiting for them. There had been a mistake. Otto was still alive. Rosa and the Meyers were so delighted they did not fully take in the rest of the courier's message.

Otto was in the maxillofacial unit at Berlin's Charité Hospital. Herr Meyer and Rosa went to visit and returned in a state of blank despair. Otto had been caught in the face by shrapnel. His top lip was missing along with most of his upper teeth and there was severe scarring on both cheeks. Although talking was possible, if you listened very carefully, Otto was not of lucid mind. *Temporary mental derangement*, the doctor had written on his record.

'Two hours' rest,' said the *Feldwebel*, when he was sure the bombardment had ceased. 'Then we dig in.'

The barn was full of soldiers but Axel and Erich managed to find a hay bale to lean against and fell asleep in seconds, resting against each other's shoulders. Barely an instant later, it seemed, there was shouting and whistle-blowing, as the *Feldwebel* roused his men. The sky was much lighter. It was almost dawn. They must have been asleep longer than they realised.

The *Feldwebel* called for silence. 'This morning we are expecting an American attack in the area. They are thousands of miles from home. They are wondering why they are here. They are soft. They have not been hardened by war. They will be easily discouraged. *You* are fighting for your Fatherland. I am sure you will defend your positions bravely.'

Then he turned to the two boys. Axel flinched, expecting to be hit for something he didn't know he'd done.

'You two, you have keen eyesight, don't you? Up the tower. Break the door down if you have to. Shout down if you see anything coming towards us.'

As they hurried to the church, Axel read the words on a wooden noticeboard by the main door. Paint was peeling off rotten wood, but he could still see *Church of St Nicholas, Aulnois* in Gothic script. So Aulnois was the name of this village. If he was to die, he at least knew where he was.

The church interior was almost as dank as the outside. There were holes in the roof and a few restless pigeons fluttered around the nave. The wooden pews had long gone. There was only a stone altar beneath a large stained-glass window, which was miraculously still intact. They tried a couple of doors before they discovered the one that led to the top of the tower.

Axel's legs ached from his night's marching as he climbed. Flat farmland stretched out before them, with a dense wood a kilometre to the north. The field in front of them was untouched by the war, aside from one large shell hole just to the right of their position. Off to the west were small villages and woods almost certainly occupied by the Tommies or the Yanks. As the day grew lighter, a thin mist began to rise. The boys peered through. 'Perfect cover, isn't it,' said Erich, then, suddenly anxious,

he asked, 'Or is it gas?' They had all seen the gas casualties back home. Men with horrible blister scars on their
faces or arms, and wheezing terribly, every breath
bubbling in corrupted lungs.

Axel felt a kind of dizzy fear as he stared across open
land into enemy territory. There in the middle and far
distance, further than the eye could see, were fields
and towns and towers and factories full of men and
women who wanted him dead. Closer, perhaps just
beyond a hedgerow, were men with bayonets and hand
grenades.

'Have you been in combat before?' asked Erich.

Axel wondered whether to lie to him, to try to seem
tougher than he was. But he realised there was no point.
As soon as they started fighting together, he would be
found out.

'No. Have you?'

Erich shook his head. Then he said, 'I had three brothers. But all of them are gone. I am the last. The last of the
Beckers.'

Axel felt a stab of pity for his new friend. 'I'll look out
for you,' he said, trying to sound braver than he felt.

'Do you miss home?' said Erich.

Axel paused to think. 'I miss my bed and three hot
meals a day. I miss Falken – our *Schäferhund* – and I miss

my brother and sister, I suppose. I don't know if I miss Wansdorf though. Do you miss Kreuzberg?'

'Yes, of course. We live in a little apartment there. My mother and father are both teachers. What about your parents?'

'My mother died,' said Axel plainly. He had learned that was the best response when he didn't want to talk about it. 'My father works on the estate – Schloss Wansdorf. He is an estate manager for the baron.'

'And you?' asked Erich. 'What did you do before this?'

'Still at school,' said Axel sheepishly. 'Like you, I imagine.'

Axel's great ambition was to be a musician – but it seemed so preposterous that he never told anyone. He wondered whether to share it with Erich now. Only his younger sister, Gretl, knew. She often listened to Axel as he played the piano. He could read music well enough, but he could also play by ear – something that Gretl seemed to think was an almost magic art.

The two boys settled into a companionable silence. Then Axel began to feel bored. He turned to Erich to ask him more about his parents, but he had gone to sleep. That was OK. The *Feldwebel* couldn't see them up here, and Axel was sure they would hear him if he came up the stairs to check on them. Besides, he could keep watch perfectly well on his own.

He tried to remember what Wansdorf was like before the war. The great celebrations every year at Christmas, Easter and the harvest festival . . . when they all feasted on delicious food. That came to an abrupt end when the war began. It was meat he missed the most. Roast pork, a succulent lamb chop, beef stew. In his last meal at home, before he left for basic training, they had eaten boiled rice pressed into a chop shape. It had a stick of wood at the side to imitate a bone, and had been fried in mutton tallow. Axel knew how difficult it was to obtain even meat substitutes like this, so he told his father it was just like eating the real thing. When the war was over, he told himself, he was going to eat lamb chops every day for a month.

He had been twelve when they heard the momentous news about the Austrian archduke – gunned down in Sarajevo by a Serbian anarchist. Barely a month later the whole of Europe was at war. Germany and Austria-Hungary against France and Russia. Even the British and their Empire had waded in against them.

There was a service in the village church before the men in the army reserve left to join the battle. The reservists stood at the front of the congregation, each wearing a special bouquet. Otto was there in the front row. Axel found it difficult singing the Bach chorale the choir-master had chosen to see them off. A great lump had risen in his throat. He wondered if Otto would be one of the ones who wouldn't come back.

Back then, everyone seemed so excited, so Axel kept his thoughts to himself. This was a war of national survival, he was told, forced upon them by powers jealous of their superior culture. Germany had a chance to prove herself. What had the Kaiser told them? They would win a 'place under the sun' – colonies like the ones the British and French were so proud of. And it would all be over by the time the leaves fell from the trees. It wasn't of course, although the first few months had gone well, with great victories against the Russians in the East.

Back then, Axel was still young enough to play with the war toys his father brought home. The model Zeppelin, the submarine, the fighter plane, the machine gun – marvels of modern technology to guarantee a German victory. He'd long grown out of playing with those toys.

Then the ration cards had arrived, the constant feeling of hunger, the cold in winter when there was no coal for the fire. Then came the news of the terrible casualties from Verdun, Ypres, the Somme, that touched every family they knew. They had given so much – even the clothes on their back – to ensure victory. At home now some people wore tatty garments made with fabric fashioned from paper and nettles and reeds. And that victory had almost arrived. Hadn't they defeated the Russians? Hadn't they won tremendous battles in Italy and Greece and Serbia? Axel couldn't understand why they were still fighting for their lives.

There was a noise behind the tower. The unmistakable sound of a body of men approaching. Axel shouted down as quietly as he could, 'Feldwebel! There are people coming behind us!'

The Feldwebel sent a soldier to investigate. The man arrived back a few moments later with a small squad of German soldiers. Caked in filth, they looked as hard as nails and had obviously been in combat for several days.

That was good, Axel supposed. More combat soldiers to help out all these new recruits. But something else worried him now. He looked down. It was quite a distance – much higher than the houses around them, even the manor, which had a grand roof with windows in the eaves. He turned to his new friend and shook him awake.

'Erich, you know this tower will be the first target for artillery, as soon as the Tommies or the Yanks realise we're here?'

CHAPTER 8

7.00 a.m.

William Franklin woke up toying with the fibre red-and-grey identity discs around his neck. He hated wearing them and remembered the fear he'd felt when he first placed them over his head. Although no one had explained it to him, it was fairly obvious that one was to remain with him if he was killed and the other was to be removed by the burial party as proof of death. Will couldn't remember which one got taken and which got left behind. But having them separated would be the start of a process that would end with a telegram to his parents. The other would stay there round his neck for the rest of eternity, unless he was blown to fragments by a high-explosive shell. Whenever he found himself thinking like that, he tried to stop it. Think of something nice, he'd say to himself, like his mum's cooking or Alice.

It was almost light now. Will had such a terrible ache in his stomach. He felt so tight and tense he could barely walk. It was like those dreams where you tried to move but found yourself paralysed. He always felt like this before combat. But then the whistle would blow and the one thing he feared more than being shot by the Germans – being shot by the Military Police – would drive him out on to the battlefield.

The rain had started in earnest. Will began his day soaked and freezing. No wonder they called them 'the poor bloody infantry'. Things usually got worse around first light when Fritz sent over a few shells. It was all part of the daily routine.

'Start the day with the prospect of dismemberment,' said Moorhouse, one of the older soldiers. 'Set the tone.' He winked when he said it though. Will was always a bit taken aback by these comments. They called it 'gallows humour' apparently.

One or two shells coming over was something he had got used to. But prolonged barrages still frightened him to death. The noise went on for ever, like perpetual thunder. Then your ears would ring for hours afterwards – you could barely hear what people said. This is what it must be like to be deaf, Will realised. He thought of his old grandad. If he ever got back to Lancaster, Will decided, he was going to be a lot more patient with him.

He reached into his pocket for his mother's latest letter. Although he was pleased to hear from her, what she wrote slightly bored him. He had been mildly interested to know that their Essex Redcomb hens, Sarah, Beth and Caitlin, had been producing at least three eggs a week. But he didn't really care how much grease his mum had managed to collect from washing-up water to give to the rag-and-bone men for use in the manufacture of explosives. And he gave even less of a fig about the patriotic parish pageant his mum and younger sister were organising for the coming Christmas celebrations. This would be the fifth wartime Christmas. When the war began, they were convinced it would be over by Christmas. Still, at least she hadn't put any nonsense in about trying to contact their Stanley with that medium she knew down the street. Lillie Franklin had been to see that woman three or four times since Stan died – wanting to know if he was 'at peace'. It made Will and Jim angry when they heard about it; the woman charged sixpence a sitting, bringing messages from 'the other side' – a day's wages for a load of waffle. Maybe his mum was still going but just kept quiet about it now.

What Will really wanted was a letter from Alice. He had written to her at least three weeks ago and that was more than enough time for her to get his letter and write back. Her last letter had been rather formal too. A lifeless description of a play they had put on for wounded men, which stopped abruptly when she reached the bottom of the page. Maybe the post was having difficulty keeping up with the army.

A couple of runners came up from the rear with flasks of tea and porridge. Just as they plonked the heavy cauldrons down, there came the first unmistakable whine of incoming shells. The men all dropped to the ground, sheltering in the ridges. Will heard the shells land but there were no great earth-shifting explosions – no tearing of the air. Instead, there was a series of jolting thuds that shook the ground, and then the eerie sound of hissing.

'Gas!' someone shouted, and the men were thrown into panic. Everyone fumbled for their respirators. The Huns had not sent gas shells over for a few weeks. Will's unit had got careless. A pair of horses were harnessed close by and their minder was desperately rummaging in two sacks on their backs, unpacking the masks the animals had to wear. In the panic, one of the men knocked over a pail of porridge. It spread over the ground like a great grey steaming cowpat.

Will had had the misfortune to be close to one of the gas shells. Too late he saw the green mist creeping towards him as it mingled with the morning fog. He got an acrid whiff of it before he could put his mask over his face and immediately began to cough. Pulling the mask on he tried to calm down and breathe as he had been instructed. But his eyes were watering and stinging terribly and he felt hot and cold despite the near-freezing morning. Worst of all, he thought he was going to be sick.

He breathed as deeply as he could through the caustic gas-mask cylinder and willed every atom in his body not to do what he knew he was about to do. It was coming up from the pit of his stomach like a great unstoppable wave. At the very last second he flipped the mask up and wretched on to the ground. A second later he pulled the mask down to take in another lungful of air, retching again immediately. He willed himself not to panic. If he inhaled his own vomit, and had another coughing fit, he would surely be dead. Fortunately he had yet to eat his breakfast and had had little to eat the previous day. It ended there. He sat down clammy with sweat as the waves of nausea gradually subsided.

There was a light wind, which helped disperse the gas, and the rain was coming down more heavily now, which also helped. Jim quickly mustered the men to get them to move away from the gas. As they left, Will saw the fellow who minded the horses lying on the ground. He thought he was dead until he began to cough in hideous spasms. The horses were wearing their masks and looked on impassively. Their minder had left it too late to put on his own. Will tore his gaze away. It was like watching a man drown before your eyes.

Will guessed the gas was chlorine or phosgene. He was grateful it hadn't been that terrible mustard gas he had heard about. That was the one that attacked your skin and eyes, blinding and blistering. He didn't want to think about what it did to your lungs.

'Fall in,' said Jim, when they had reconvened several hundred yards down the road. 'Lieutenant Richardson wants to have a word with you all.'

The men waited in their ranks, while Jim went to tell the lieutenant his soldiers were ready. He hurried over, anxious to have kept them waiting. That was nice of him, thought Will. He had known officers who would keep their men waiting for ten or fifteen minutes and then stroll over without a care in the world.

Will looked at the platoon lieutenant in his officer's outfit. It all seemed too big for him. He wondered if Richardson's parents had minded spending all that money on the Sam Browne belt and the short sword. Front-line officers, it was well known, had the briefest life expectancy. Will felt sorry for him, and admiration too. Richardson had moved heaven and earth to get them hot rations, and held regular foot inspections to ensure none of them developed infections. It was quite a thing for a young man, barely more than a boy, to command the respect of these men. Will knew Jim thought well of Richardson too.

'I have just heard from Divisional Command,' their lieutenant told them in a loud, clear voice. Richardson knew how to address a squad of soldiers with clarity and confidence. 'We are to attack the town of Saint-Libert to the east of this position at ten ack emma, following a half-hour artillery bombardment. As you know, we have American soldiers stationed on the other side of the woods to our right and they will also be attacking the adjacent village of Aulnois at around the same time. We are expecting light resistance but I would urge you all to show caution and not to risk your life unnecessarily. Prior to the attack I have asked Sergeant Franklin to take a small group of volunteers to these woods to the south of here, to check they are clear of enfilade fire or any other enemy activity that would hinder our advance. I also urge you to be prepared for further gas attacks. The bombardment this morning resulted in the loss of Private Atherton, who died gallantly saving the horses in his care. I would remind you all that, even though we may cherish and care for the packhorses, they are not worth the life of a trained soldier. Thank you. Rest easy.'

The men were issued with hot coffee – or something approaching it. Jim came and sat down next to Will. 'I'd like you to come with me,' he whispered. 'I want to keep an eye on you. And if you volunteer it'll impress the others. Make them think you're not shirking. So if I'm easy on you later, they'll be more likely to let it go.'

'Is it going to be dangerous?' asked Will.

'Who knows?' said Jim. 'Fritz probably won't have men in the forest. But going in there to look will probably be safer than taking part in a frontal assault on the town.'

Will nodded. When Jim stood up soon after to ask for his patrol volunteers, his younger brother was the first to raise his hand. Other men followed suit.

'We'll set out in half an hour,' said Jim. 'Leave your packs here. You'll just need your weapons.'

Just then, Richardson came up to Jim and leaned forward to whisper in his ear. He got up and left the other men on their own. Will suspected the lieutenant had asked Jim to help him with his letter to the parents of Private Atherton.

Jim had told Will that Richardson had the same formula for every letter. Regardless of the usual gruesome circumstances, he would say the man died quickly from a shot to the head, or a shell blast that killed him in an instant. He even told the parents of the men who had been shot for cowardice that they had been killed on the battlefield. That was a kindness no one could argue against.

And Richardson would also say he had been well liked by his comrades, even if he was a constant whiner or a shirker. 'I try to dissuade him sometimes,' Jim told Will, 'especially if the man was a bloody pain in the backside. I'll say, "He was a sour old sod, sir. His mum won't recognise your description." But Richardson always says, "Can't kick a man when he's down, eh, Sergeant?" and he'll insist we keep it. I'm not sure that's right. If you know your husband or your son's one of life's miseries, then hearing they were the life and soul of the party is going to make you wonder if they really did die as quickly as you've been told.'

Will wondered what Richardson would write about Atherton. He kept himself to himself. The men had often joked that he liked the horses more than his human comrades.

When Jim returned, Will's squad were sitting round a

wood fire bare-chested, going through the daily ritual of delousing their shirts. The fire was blazing away, but it was still a freezing business. You roasted at the front, froze on your back.

How to get the lice out of his shirt was one of the first things Will had learned when he came over to France. His 'Special Preparation Against Vermin In The Trenches', from Boots the Chemist, had been useless. Destroying lice was far more complicated than simply rubbing ointment into your uniform. Along with his rifle and ammunition and iron rations, they'd been issued with a candle. One of the lads had joked, 'What's this for? Romantic dinners?' He'd been put on a charge for that. They soon found out. The only thing that got rid of lice was fire. You lit the candle and then ran the flame over the seams, the places where the lice gathered in their hundreds. There was quite a skill to it, killing the lice without setting your shirt alight, or singeing it so badly the material ripped when you put it on. You knew you'd killed them because they exploded with a little pop. When the men were all sitting together, doing their delousing, it was almost like a miniature machine gun going off.

As they formed up for the forest patrol, Will looked around at the other volunteers. There was Ogden and

Binney, who had both come out with him in the spring. Before they had boarded the train down to the Harwich ferry, they had all been issued with live ammunition, and Ogden had actually leaned out of the window and taken potshots at farm animals with his Lee-Enfield rifle. Will had seen a scraggy old sheep topple over and had gone and remonstrated with him. It took a whole month before Ogden forgave him. Will was pleased to see Weale and Moorhouse and another veteran of 1914, Hosking, were coming. The three of them thought themselves invincible, and no wonder. Will knew boys, and a few officers, who had died in their first hour at the Front. Cowell and Bradshaw, two other old hands, who had been at the Front for a couple of years, were with them too.

'Hosking, take point, watch out for mines, any booby traps, but most of all, we're looking for snipers. If they've got machine guns on the edge of the forest, we'll find out soon enough, so don't bunch up.'

Sergeant Franklin had his stern voice on.

'No talking, no smoking, you know the drill. You want to tell me something, you come and tap me on the shoulder. All right? And whisper.'

Will looked at the men they were leaving behind and felt himself lucky. He was sure Jim was right. The forest patrol was definitely a safer bet than the attack on the village. They set off and within ten minutes the dense green trees loomed up before them.

Shortly after they left, the soldiers preparing for the assault were surprised to see a young runner from Divisional Command arrive breathlessly among them. He seemed to be bursting with a wonderful secret, grinning from ear to ear. He could barely contain himself when he asked for Lieutenant Richardson. He handed over an envelope, which the young officer immediately ripped open. The anxiety on his face vanished in an instant. He too seemed strangely excited, and called for the men to assemble immediately. He even rushed around their position himself, to ensure every man under his command would be present to hear him.

Eventually, when he had gathered them all together, he announced, 'Men, I have some momentous news. The attack on Saint-Libert has been called off.' A murmur of relief went around the platoon. 'In fact, I have been informed that hostilities will cease at eleven o'clock this morning.'

Lieutenant Richardson's men looked at him with dull acceptance. There was no cheer, no celebration, no throwing caps into the air. He felt a flash of exasperation. 'Gentlemen, don't you understand? The war is over.'

'Very good, sir,' said Corporal Entwistle, who took on Jim's role when he was elsewhere. The men remained impassive. It was as if Richardson had just announced that breakfast was being served half an hour later.

'Sir, what about Sergeant Franklin's patrol,' said Entwistle.

'Send a man to fetch them back, Corporal. Tell him to get a move on.'

Half a mile away a couple of shells screamed down and exploded. Even from that distance they still shook the ground around them. 'The war's not over yet, sir,' said the corporal and marched briskly over to Rifleman Heaton.

Corporal Entwistle had never liked Heaton. He was always too eager to obey the officers, always happy to volunteer. There was something smarmy about him. And those books he read – always fishing out an E.M. Forster or a James Joyce from his knapsack when they stopped for a break. That was all right for an officer. But Heaton's father was a blacksmith. He had no business with books like that. He had just fished one out to read now. Corporal Entwistle pulled down the book and peered straight into his face. 'Make yourself useful, lad. Go and fetch

Sergeant Franklin and his patrol and tell them the war is over.'

Heaton immediately put down his book and gathered up his rifle and helmet. 'Yes, Corporal. Which direction did they go?'

'Just follow the path there into the woods, son. Make it sharpish.'

Heaton headed off as fast as he could, in the stooped posture which had become second nature to him. Like the others in the platoon, he was too exhausted to feel anything other than a kind of dull surprise about the end of the war. Maybe when they'd stopped the infernal artillery bombardment he could hear in the distance, maybe then he'd feel something. For now, that endless rumble just clouded up his mind.

As Heaton approached the wood, the artillery stopped and there was no small arms fire – not entirely unheard of, but rare anywhere on the Western Front. He could even hear a few birds singing and began to walk in a more upright manner.

He thought about what he was going to do when he got home, and the terrible row he would have with his father when he announced that he wanted to study to go to college. Heaton wanted to be a teacher. English literature. It was the thing he loved the most. Far in the distance he thought he could see a group of soldiers. He called out, 'Sergeant Franklin,' but they were too far away to hear. He called again to no avail and had began to run towards them when a sniper's bullet caught him square on the forehead, throwing him off his feet and twisting him round as he fell. Private Heaton was dead before his body collapsed like a discarded doll on to the ground.

CHAPTER 9

8.00 a.m.

Eddie Hertz slept late – a rare luxury as he was often up before first light to fly the dawn patrol. Today he was off the roster. As he came to, the first thing he noticed was the scent of Céline's perfume and he felt a stab of loneliness.

Eddie didn't really believe her scarf would keep him safe, but he liked the idea of having something of hers so close to him. His fellow pilots were crazy about their rituals and superstitions. Some of them even took a cat up with them. Biederbeck had a black one – the classic witch's familiar – but Eddie thought it was cruel to the poor animal. What would happen if it got stuck under your feet or was so terrified it wanted to jump out?

He threw on his clothes and splashed his face at the basin by the window. It was a short walk to the mess at the airbase, and if he hurried he'd be in time for breakfast.

Biederbeck was there, still in his flying gear, black soot on his face with an incongruous white patch around his eyes where he had removed his goggles.

'Hey, Eddie,' he shouted over. 'Guess what I've been up to!' He looked exceedingly pleased with himself.

'Another notch on the propeller, huh?' said Eddie. 'Was it a Fokker? What does your cat think about that?'

'Better than that, pal! I got one of those ammunition trains. About two in the morning. Saw it coming into this little town near to Mons. The smoke in the moonlight gave it away – so I came in low and dropped a couple of twenty-five-pounders. I'd like to tell you it was my skill and judgement –' he winked, a habit Eddie was beginning to find irritating – 'but I got lucky. Very lucky. The bombs had their usual delay, and as I was flying away I heard an explosion, then about ten seconds later the whole thing erupted like a volcano. The crate felt like it had been picked up by a wave. If I'd been just above, I'd have been fried along with all the Huns below.

'Course, I circled around to check out the damage. Bright as day it was for a while. Then some of the Huns started on me with machine guns so I got out of there pretty damn quick.'

'So you're the one who disturbed my good night's sleep,' said Eddie.

Their conversation was interrupted by another airman, who burst into the mess with a delighted expression on his face. 'Hold the front page, fellas. I got the scoop of the century!'

Biederbeck and Eddie looked at him expectantly. 'War's over!' he announced breathlessly. 'The whole shooting match ends at eleven o'clock this morning. Ceasefire!'

The mess erupted in a great cheer. 'We're done, boys. We're all going to live,' said one of the pilots.

Eddie cheered along with the rest of them. But something was bothering him. As he ate his bacon and scrambled eggs, he felt a twinge of disappointment. He'd got four Huns. You needed five to call yourself an ace. He'd love to go back home and have his picture in the paper: *Eddie Hertz – fighter ace*. That would make Janie Holland wish she hadn't dumped him.

'I'm going out to bag myself a Hun,' he told Biederbeck.

'Squadron leader won't allow it, Eddie. There's no operations now for the rest of the day.'

Another pilot leaned over from the next table. 'That attack they told us about at yesterday's briefing – Colonel Miller's 91st Division. Going in at Aulnois this morning.'

Eddie looked blank. Then he remembered. 'Ten o'clock, isn't it?'

'I'd guess they could do with some air support,' said the pilot.

'They'll call that assault off surely,' said Eddie, suddenly feeling deflated.

The pilot shook his head. 'Not if I know that bastard Miller. He'll be wanting to milk every last chance he's got to chase the Hun. Those men will fight right up to the last minute.'

Eddie nodded. 'I'm gonna get my erks to fuel her up and I'm going out. They can throw the book at me when I get back.' 'Erk' was bit of slang they'd picked up from the Royal Flying Corps. It was an abbreviation of sorts, of 'aircraftman' – the mechanics that kept a plane airworthy.

He ran over to the barn that served as a temporary hangar for three of the squadron's Sopwith Camels. 'Hey, fellas,' he shouted over to a couple of men in overalls who sat playing cards in the corner. 'Get her fuelled up. I'm going out in fifteen.'

The ground crew leaped to their feet. They had heard there would be no more flying that morning. But Eddie was the boss. If he said he was going up, he was going up.

Eddie hurried to the farmhouse, grabbed his flying jacket and Céline's scarf and hurriedly pulled on his calf-length brown boots. His flying helmet and leather gloves were waiting for him on the seat of his Camel. He looked out at the overcast grey sky and quickly pulled on a thick woollen sweater. It was going to be cold up there.

Leaving without so much as a final glance, he ran towards the Camel. The ground crew were finishing off the fuelling. 'Give us five more minutes, boss. Then she's ready to go.'

Whenever Eddie climbed into the wicker seat of his Camel, he had the strangest mixture of feelings. Always excitement – that, at least, had never left him, but fear too – a queasy nausea whenever he smelled the oil and gasoline and polished metal of the engine. That magnificent piece of gleaming machinery that whirred and popped and hammered with such precision right in front of his eyes, this extraordinary device that lifted him above the clouds, could also deliver him to a horrible burning death or crush his flesh and bones if he crashed to the ground. Flying was a Faustian pact. You had the chance to go up into the air and soar like a bird – but you also faced the fate that British song so vividly promised.

The drill for take-off was so ingrained Eddie ran through it without really thinking what he was doing.

Engine checks, machine gun checks, two twenty-five-pound bombs right underneath him on the underside of the fuselage. Eddie didn't like having those things on board. If he crashed on take-off, or got hit, who could say they wouldn't go off?

'OK, let's get her off. Contact!' said Eddie, and the mechanic swung the varnished wooden propeller. The engine spluttered into life with a spurt of blue exhaust, and his nostrils filled with the smell of petrol. And as it usually did on the first time, the prop came to an abrupt halt and had to be spun again. As it usually did, this time the rotary engine fired on all nine of its cylinders and Eddie felt an intoxicating power judder through the small biplane. It was like a great beast pulling on a leash.

That engine had terrified him when he first flew these Camels. The way it spun on its housing – this great lump of gleaming steel whizzing around at 1,500 revolutions per minute. It was like a great big gyroscope and it perpetually tugged the flimsy, wood-and-canvas plane off to the right. If you weren't careful, that engine would be the death of you. And Eddie was convinced that crashing with the thing spinning around like that was far more dangerous than crashing with a stationary in-line engine.

But without it, the Camel wouldn't be half the plane it was. Nothing did a right turn as quickly as a Camel, as many a German pilot had found out to their cost. Left turns were slower – laborious really. But the aircraft was agile, and that was what made it so formidable in a dogfight. If you could cope with its limitations – sluggish above 12,000 feet, slow compared to the latest German Fokkers – you were lucky to have one.

Take-off was the most dangerous time. A full fuel tank added to the forward weight of the craft and Eddie always felt anxious until the wheels left the ground and the shaking stopped. He gunned the engine, feeling it straining on its housing.

'Chocks away,' shouted Eddie, and made the usual gesture. He didn't know why he even shouted. The noise drowned everything out. The ground crew spun the Camel on its spindly wheels, holding on to its tail, safely away from that roaring engine. The machine emerged from the barn and Eddie began to trundle along the bumpy grass to the runway.

Checking wind direction, and making sure he had maximum length for take-off, Eddie gave the engine a final gunning and then began his run. The wind started to sing in the struts and he could feel the terrific power of the machine at his fingertips.

This manoeuvre required supreme concentration, working the ailerons, elevators and rudder with hands and feet, and pushing the throttle just so. The torque was phenomenal. As Eddie gained speed, the whole aircraft was wrenched to the right. He set the stick and the pedals to counteract that swing and pulled back the throttle.

If he got this wrong, he could easily find himself in a high-speed collision with a tree, and then they really would have to take the cylinder out of his kidneys, and all the other grisly things from that song. Eddie had seen enough Camels leap in the air, only to stall and land with a sickening explosion, or worst of all tip forward, shattering the propeller and engine housing and mangling the pilot . . . it was all too easy to do.

He felt the tail lift. This was the trickiest part. Keeping her level for a few seconds more. His eyes darted down to the speedometer. It was at 70 mph. He pulled back the stick and the jolting stopped as he parted company with the ground. Immediately, his anxiety vanished. He climbed to the low cloud base, keen to break out into the vast blue domain above. He could feel the moisture of the heavy clouds in his throat and sensed their clammy coldness on his face.

Five minutes later he was through and basking in brilliant sunshine. The thrill of that never left him. Those mere mortals down on the ground – they had to put up with whatever weather the heavens decreed. A pilot could enjoy the sunshine whenever he took to the sky.

And the clouds up there. Some of them were as big as mountains – with craggy promontories and great gullies. And when you got really high up, you could see the cloud fields stretch to the horizon. You could even see the curve of the Earth.

Being able to do that made Eddie feel like a god. And the girls loved him. Even in New York, in the week before he left, they had flocked to hear his news. All the most glamorous girls went for the flyboys – especially the fighter pilots. They were the princes of the sky. Eddie enjoyed the attention, but he was wise enough to know how shallow it all was.

Now he had reached 1,000 feet, just above the cloud base. He turned the nose of his Camel to the east and the enemy.

CHAPTER 10

8.45 a.m.

'No talking,' whispered Sergeant Franklin, 'and watch where you step. I don't want any falling over and giving us away to a sniper. You never know who might be in here. Hosking, you stay on point for now; I'll be right behind you.'

Will watched the others respond. With some of the other sergeants and corporals the men would exchange glances, even look askance at their orders. Jim's commands were met only by stern nods and brief murmurs of agreement. He noticed how the men would often bunch around Jim, as if being close to their sergeant offered them extra protection.

Jim checked in his pocket and brought out a small compass. 'Any of you got one of these?' he asked. 'No? Then make sure you keep with me. It's very easy to lose your direction in a wood, especially where it's dense.'

Hosking took the lead without a word and the nine of

them began to advance into the great green-and-brown shelter of the forest. The evergreens and deciduous trees made for a beautiful mixture. Some of the deciduous ones had shed now, with only a few tattered leaves remaining. But the evergreens offered dense cover for anyone who might be watching.

One by one they were swallowed by the forest, and Will immediately felt a chill as he moved into its shadow. How strange, he thought, that such a place of natural beauty should suddenly become so sinister. Will loved the woods back home in the Lune Valley – he'd spent half his childhood playing in them. He and his mates had built dens in the dense vegetation or hollowed-out tree trunks, and even camped out for the night. Being here, in such similar terrain, filled him with a sadness he could not immediately understand.

The early-morning mist had turned to a dank fog, which hung around the lower branches. There was a strange smell too, which Will recognised as gas. Not the intense, choking smell that came from a recently fallen shell, but the faint remains of an earlier attack. Will hated that mixture – fog and gas. From a distance it was difficult to tell, but the closer you got, the more you could make out the green tendrils in the grey fog.

Now the cold was getting to him. He began to fantasise

about a proper breakfast. Bacon, eggs, sausages, two lovely crisp fried eggs done in butter. He was never going to eat porridge again in his life. His stomach gave a gurgle, so loud Ogden looked around and winked at him. But as he did so he tripped and fell to the ground with a clatter of belt buckles, rifle strap and rustling brown leaves.

Sergeant Franklin looked round with cold disapproval. Ogden would be on latrine duty as soon as they got back.

As they ventured further into the dark depths, an enormous shape loomed out of the trees, making Will shudder. A German warplane had crashed, and hung nose down in the bare branches of a great oak. It had been there for a few months now, by the look of it. The canvas fuselage was starting to decay, and green moss was growing along the bare wooden struts where the fabric had been torn away. Will looked at the cockpit and was relieved to see it was empty. He'd seen pilots leap from burning machines, preferring a crushing fall to a fiery death. This machine was burned up, with black soot and charred fabric around the engine and along the side of the cockpit. Maybe that's what had happened here.

Even in its derelict state the machine still had a fascinating beauty. The propeller hub, with the splintered stubs of its blades, was painted with a bright red spiral, which matched the colour of the fuselage. Great black crosses adorned the wings and tail. British warplanes were never so gaudy. But now it looked like an immense bird of prey that had been hung upside down as a trophy.

The men all stared at this extraordinary sight. In the middle distance a bombardment started – shells falling in the far end of the forest at regular intervals, blue flashes filtering through the dense vegetation. The explosions seemed muffled, but they were still close enough to feel through the ground.

'If they're ours, someone needs a right bollocking,' said Jim under his breath. 'If they're Fritz's, then it means there's none of their men in the forest. If they start falling any closer, we'll move out.'

As they left the great carcass of the warplane, another sound disturbed them. Will looked up to see a plane flying overhead, so close he could clearly make out the white discs on the wheels of the undercarriage. It was a Yank. Will suppressed an urge to wave; he would never see him under the thick canopy of the wood.

Flying seemed such an extraordinary thing to him – to be able to take to the fresh blue sky and leave the squalor and the soggy cold behind, the trudging through mud, and the sleeping in barns or out in the open.

What he would give to be able to go back to a base every night to sleep in a proper bed. Pilots seemed like mythical figures to Will. Earlier in the war, when he was still young enough to be taken in by those stories, he had read about the French ace Guynemer, who had flown so high he had been taken by the angels, or the English hero Albert Ball, who was said to have flown into a cloud and vanished. But Will had seen the burned-out skeletons of flying machines scattered around the battlefield, and occasionally the charred bodies of luckless pilots, and he remembered another story he'd been told at school, of Icarus the ancient Greek, flying too close to the sun, and he decided he might be safer down on the ground after all.

As the engine note faded and they began to delve further into the forest, Weale held up his hand for them to stop and listen. 'Where are Binney and Moorhouse?' he whispered.

'I were just thinking that,' said Jim. 'Don't tell me they've scarpered.'

The patrol retraced their steps. The two missing soldiers, who had been at the end of their line, were close by the plane, where they had all stopped to look. Binney lay on his side on the ground, as if asleep. Will noticed how smooth his face was. It was all too easy to imagine him as a young boy, waiting for his mother to come and kiss him goodnight.

Moorhouse was lying on his back. His eyes were open. He looked surprised.

They had both been shot through the head. Moorhouse was obviously dead, but Jim went over to Binney to check for a pulse. He shook his head. Weale knelt over Moorhouse's body and closed his eyes. 'Poor sod. Four years of this,' he said to no one in particular. 'Four years.'

All at once Will felt a knot tighten in his gut. 'We never even heard anything.'

'He must have timed his shots with the artillery barrage,' whispered Jim. 'Clever bastard. Well, he's stirred up some trouble for himself.'

He gathered his patrol together. Will could see the others felt as shaken as he was. 'There's a sniper here who's firing whenever the shells drop. When you hear a shell, dive for cover – that's when he's going to fire. And when he cocks it up – he's bound to mistime one, then that's when we'll get him.'

Jim went over to the bodies again to collect the men's identity tags. Then he said, 'I'll take point. Franklin, you take second.' Will always took a moment to register when Jim called him by his surname. But he liked the idea of being behind Jim, peering through the forest, looking out for signs, protecting his older brother.

Sergeant Franklin's courage had given the men heart. A single sniper and a patrol. The odds were in their favour. He was probably up a tree somewhere. Once they heard him they'd hunt him down.

CHAPTER 11

9.30 a.m.

High in his evergreen perch, a sniper watches the patrol. Despite the cold morning fog, he is sticky with sweat. He calculates his chances. In the silence, there are too many to pick off in a quick brace of shots. At the first bullet they would scatter and hunt him down. He must wait for the shells to fall, and then he can strike. If there are no more shells, then he must come down from his eyrie and shoot from a position that allows him retreat. He has been doing this for six months now. Every day brings further peril. But he has convinced himself that if he is careful, he has a greater chance of surviving than an ordinary infantryman. Being a sniper lets him gauge his own risks and he alone is responsible for his actions. Unlike the infantry. If they are ordered to charge to almost certain death, then they have no option. He is a lone wolf. Picking off the stray sheep.

He waits another ten minutes. There are no more artillery barrages. He decides he must stalk the Tommies, rather than wait for them. Slowly, agonisingly slowly, he begins to descend from the treetop. There is a dip in the ground close to the eastern end of the forest – near his own lines. He will hide in there and kill as many of them as fate allows, then retreat.

He is fleet-footed and sure in his sense of direction. As the British soldiers comb through the northern side of the forest, he reaches the spot he remembers and quickly gathers together twigs, branches, brushwood, to hide his position and, most especially, the flash of his rifle.

He hears the patrol in the distance. They are good. They make barely a sound. But a group of men in a forest cannot help but give themselves away. The swish of feet in bracken. The crisp footfalls on dead leaves and brittle twigs. They are coming his way. The one in charge, the one with the great bristling moustache and the stripes on his tunic, he is at the front of the line. Perfect. Cut off the head and the body will cease to function. He studies them through the telescopic sight of his Mauser 98, waiting for them to come into range. Maybe he can get two shots off. The sergeant and the younger fellow behind him. They look similar enough to be related. Perhaps they are brothers. Is it right to deprive a mother of two sons in a single day? He thinks of his own mother, who lost her two youngest on the Marne, and his finger tightens on the trigger. On impulse he switches his target. The young one first, then as the older one turns he will kill him too. That way there will be less chance of detection. He studies his target. He is no more than a boy, but his two younger brothers were barely a year or so older. He breathes deeply, preparing for his shot, and shivers involuntarily as a cold wind blows over his position.

Something catches in his throat. He stifles the urge to cough. Too late he recognises the bitter taste. Gas, from an earlier bombardment. Most of it has dissipated, but a few pockets still linger in the hollows of the forest. The urge to cough is irresistible, and the more he coughs the more he breathes in – his lungs fill with chlorine. His eyes are streaming now, he is retching and bent double in breathless agony.

Sergeant Franklin hears the man and signals for Ogden and Weale to investigate. They run towards the sound and recognise their quarry in an instant. Blackened face, helmet and uniform covered in leaves and bracken. It is the sniper. He looks at them with desperate, pleading eyes, coughing blood and phlegm. Ogden levels his rifle to shoot, but Weale pulls on his arm and shakes his head. A shot might draw the attention of other snipers.

Poor dead Moorhouse has been his pal for the whole wretched war. Weale lunges forward, a livid rage coursing through his body, and clubs the choking man to death with the butt of his rifle.

CHAPTER 12

9.30 a.m.

High above their heads Eddie Hertz checked his compass
and settled into his flight path. This close to the Front
you could expect to be attacked at any time after you took
off. Or even as you were taking off. That was how he had
got his second 'kill', three months ago. They were strafing
a Hun aerodrome and this bright red Fokker was taking
off. Just one on his own, the brave little bastard, coming
up to meet the whole squadron. Eddie was flying over
and the craft came into his line of fire – tail up, just ready
to leave the ground. Eddie let off a long burst from his
machine guns. He was close enough to see the pilot's
head jerk back as the bullets tore into him, and he
swerved away as the Fokker leaped into the air. The pilot
must have pulled the stick back when the bullets hit. The
plane flew up twenty feet then stalled, crashing to the
ground and bursting into flames. Eddie saw the pyre he
had created and felt a fleeting elation. But that wore off

quick enough. It wasn't very 'sporting', was it, shooting a man as he tried to take off? It was too easy.

The next kill, three days later, was a damn sight more deserving. That was a day he was really proud of. The story had even made *The New York Times*. That had been back in August. Eddie and two of his squadron, Flight Commander Doyle Bridgman and Lieutenant Irvin Dwight, had been close to the Front when Bridgman had spotted a Hun observation plane low down on the horizon: a twin-engine Rumpler by the look of it, little more than a black dot skirting to and fro along the edge of the clouds. They had screamed down and made short work of the two-seater plane. Bridgman had fired the only shots needed to kill the crew and see the clumsy plane nosedive down to the pockmarked mud below.

But this was a short-lived victory. These observation planes were often there as bait, and as the patrol regained height Eddie suddenly heard the *rat-a-tat* of machine guns and saw glowing tracer bullets curve past his plane. At once they were surrounded by brightly coloured Fokkers. The four Hun fighter planes had come in straight out of the sun – just as American pilots had been warned in their training manuals. Eddie's flight commander was in trouble. Bridgman had been wounded, that much was apparent, and his Camel was banking over to the right. Eddie could see him slumped against the side of his cockpit. He wondered if he was already dead. But then his engine caught and the man began to rouse himself, leaning forward in his cockpit to beat at the flames with one hand. Black smoke thickened, and he began to cough in great heaving spasms. The flying machine lurched sharply to the right and Eddie knew he would never see Doyle Bridgman again.

A Fokker screamed past him and Eddie immediately noticed bullet holes in the fabric of his right wing. Pushing his stick down, he wheeled his Camel into a tight right turn and searched the sky for his opponents. The odds were not good. Four Huns against him and Dwight. And this kind of Fokker, the D.VIII, was well matched with the Camels.

Eddie was too low. Too low to make an escape back to his own lines if his engine was hit and failed, too low to have any tactical advantage over his attackers. Pulling the Camel into a climb he desperately scanned the sky. He banked left, then right, but they were still nowhere to be seen. Irvin Dwight had vanished as well. Had they got him too?

The rattle of machine-gun fire and the spatter of bullets hitting canvas caught him by surprise. Even over the roar of the engine he could hear it. Two Fokkers screamed past again to his right. Eddie knew his luck was running out. Two passes, two hits on his machine. Next time, he was sure, he would be riddled with bullets. As he looked down, he saw both the Fokkers taking a tight right turn, in close formation. He jerked his control column and flew to meet them head on. This was a manoeuvre neither of the German pilots was expecting. Eddie started to fire, well before he was in effective range, but the sight of his tracer bullets hurtling towards them must have unnerved one of his opponents, because the right-hand plane immediately veered to the left. It was a disastrous move. Catching his fellow pilot on the wing, his propeller sheered off great chunks of wood and fabric, and both planes began to plummet to earth. Eddie pulled his stick back, climbing out of the path of the two aircraft.

The plane that had been hit was doomed. Its starboard wing now barely half its normal length, it dropped from the sky. The one that had crashed into it was luckier. Although its propeller had been lost, the plane was still airworthy, and the pilot put it in a steep dive to build up speed and enable him to glide to earth.

Eddie wondered if he should chase the blighter and finish him off. But there were other German planes to worry about. He decided to leave the man to his fate. If he survived, he would have to live with the shame of his clumsy manoeuvre.

Banking swiftly to port, Eddie could see two, no, three planes a thousand feet below. It was Dwight, he was sure of it, pursued by the two other Fokkers. The odds were even now. Eddie took his Camel into a steep downward curve and within moments he was close behind the two German planes. He kept expecting them to veer off, but neither pilot seemed to have noticed him. Maybe they had assumed their comrades had shot him down. They were closing in on Dwight, and certain of a kill. The lead Fokker began to fire his guns, and Eddie decided he could wait no longer. Although he was still out of effective range, he pressed the trigger on his two Vickers machine guns and sprayed the sky with bullets and tracer.

He had arrived too late to help Irvin Dwight. As he flew closer, Eddie could see Dwight's plane peppered with bullets from nose to tail and the pilot slumped forward in his cockpit. Eddie changed his target, aiming now at the lead Fokker and cutting a long burst into the centre of the airplane. He guessed he had caught the pilot completely unawares because he took no evasive action. Eddie's shots hit home, and the engine immediately caught. Within a few seconds the entire front was enveloped in flame. Eddie cried out in savage glee as the plane set into a deep dive, smearing the sky with oily black smoke. Now there were just two of them left. One to one.

The final Fokker had vanished again. Eddie hurriedly searched around and found him soon enough. He was climbing, maybe a quarter of a mile ahead. Eddie gave chase, the two planes circling in great wide arcs all alone in the vast blue canopy of the sky. There were few clouds in this sector, and Eddie was certain he would catch this fellow if he kept on his tail.

He looked around, anxious that he should not be jumped by more German fighters but there was no one else there. His opponent had made a fatal tactical error. The Camel and the D.VIII were well matched in speed and armament, but the Camel could go a couple of thousand feet higher. If the Fokker kept climbing, Eddie would eventually get above him and then the German pilot would be at his mercy.

Soon Eddie was flying at a height he rarely reached. His opponent was still there in front of him. Eddie steeled himself to keep his eyes firmly on the aircraft ahead and not become distracted by the great panorama below. He was so high now he could see past the wasteland of the Western Front, beyond the pockmarked mud, the livid scars of the trenches, to greener land beyond.

It was getting really cold now, and Eddie noticed how deeply he was having to breathe. His engine was struggling too, beginning to splutter. He was finding it difficult to stay focused on his quarry. He wondered if the Hun pilot was having the same problem with lack of oxygen at this altitude. He adjusted his fuel mixture and hoped his Camel would not let him down.

Perhaps it was a momentary loss of concentration, or even consciousness, but all at once Eddie could no longer see his enemy. Willing himself to raise his body up and further into the freezing slipstream, he leaned over his cockpit and spotted him. The Fokker was making a steep dive towards the German lines. Eddie waited until his opponent was slightly below his height, then turned his Camel and pulled his throttle to its full extent. The engine screamed in its housing, and the struts began to sing as the small plane strained against the forces of momentum and gravity. Eddie worried that the bullet holes in his wing might have fatally damaged the canvas, but his erks had done a good maintenance job. As far as he could tell, there was no tearing of fabric, and the Camel's airframe seemed to be holding up to this punishing treatment.

As he closed in on the Fokker, Eddie prepared to fire his guns. He was low on ammunition now, he reckoned, so this time he would wait until he was well within range.

The German pilot was certainly not making it easy for him. Whenever Eddie lined up for a shot, the Fokker veered off to the left or right. It took four attempts for Eddie to finally get close enough to the German plane to be able to follow him into his turns and dives, and by then the altimeter told him they were down to five thousand feet.

Eddie was level behind the Fokker when he unleashed his bullets. The tracer shots showed him he had found his target and immediately he had to veer sharply right to avoid being hit by debris peeling off the stricken plane. The Fokker slowed down as its engine spluttered and stopped, and Eddie sped ahead, fearing he might fly in front of his foe and allow him to fire his own guns. But the pilot had enough on his mind.

The Fokker's nose dropped and it dived towards the ground. Once more above his opponent, Eddie followed him down. There was no smoke, no flames. He wondered whether to fire again, but he couldn't see the point. The Fokker was gliding now. He could see its stationary propeller. His opponent would be lucky to survive his landing.

Eddie could see hedgerows and lanes below, and the German pilot was trying to line up his machine to land on a straight empty road through the middle of a field. Eddie circled, wondering where they were. He guessed they were several miles behind the German lines – certainly somewhere as yet untouched by fighting.

The Hun was going to do it – he was flying above the road, and gently placed his Fokker down, coasting for a couple of hundred yards or so as the powerless machine lost momentum. In a flash Eddie realised he had missed his 'kill'. Once the engine had been repaired the machine would still be flight-worthy. The pilot might have been injured, but he couldn't have been that badly hurt to execute such a good dead-stick landing.

What was stopping him strafing the plane on the ground and killing the pilot? Should he do it? Two kills in one day. That would impress the girls back home, and the stuffed shirts at Yale. Eddie decided he would do it. Hell, all was fair in love and war, they kept saying. Maybe this bastard would have done the same to him, and two of his pals had just slaughtered Bridgman and Dwight. He turned the Camel into a tight curve, feeling himself pressed hard into his seat, and flew low towards his target. As he approached, he could see the Hun nimbly leaping from the cockpit. Eddie thought he was going to run for his life. Good. Then he could destroy the machine at least, and claim his kill. But the pilot didn't run; he stood there by the wing, stiffly to attention, and saluted. You won, he seemed to be saying, and I respect you. That was it. Eddie pulled back the control stick and waggled his wings as he flew over. He wasn't going to kill a man like that.

As he climbed into the sky, he noticed the scar of the Western Front to the west. It was time to head for home.

He landed to a hero's welcome – the squadron carrying him back to the mess on their shoulders, but not before his aircrew had told him his Camel had fifty-eight bullet holes in it. One of them had almost severed a control wire to his ailerons. The steel wire was barely held by a thread. If that had gone, then he would have lost control of his plane and almost certainly plunged into a fatal spiral.

'We thought you'd bought it with Dwight and Bridgman,' said his erk. 'We'd heard about them already. Bridgman crashed behind the British lines. Dwight came down just inside Hunland. And reports on the ground say you got three Huns.'

Eddie couldn't lie. When he presented his flight report and claimed his kill, he told his squadron leader that two of the Fokkers had crashed into each other, and one had definitely gone down. The fourth had escaped with a dead-stick landing.

'Bad luck, Hertz,' he said. 'As your commanding officer, I'm duty bound to tell you I would have polished him off on the way down,' he said with a wink, 'or got him on the ground, but I suppose your guns jammed, eh?'

Eddie nodded and laughed. He wasn't going to tell his CO the story about the saluting pilot. But he wondered again if he should have shot him and destroyed the plane.

That night in the mess, as they celebrated his return and his third victory with a bottle of champagne, Eddie raised a glass to propose a toast to his absent friends Dwight and Bridgman, and felt a pang of admiration for the German pilot he had outwitted. He wished all aerial combat could end like that.

Since then he had mainly flown infantry support missions – shooting up the Huns on the ground as they fled before the might of the Allies, who seemed unstoppable now. All the way to Berlin. The landscapes had changed. When he first arrived, it was all bombed-out farmhouses and villages, great pockmarked landscapes and charcoal trees. Now the Germans were retreating through fresh countryside which had been untouched by war for four years.

And that sort of action didn't seem very sporting either. Eddie knew some of the pilots thought it was funny to shoot at fleeing men. When they boasted about it in the officer's mess, they would imitate the actions of terrified soldiers, running here and there in blind panic, and laugh. Those sorts of men loved to shoot up troop trains too – watch the locomotive explode in a great geyser of compressed steam, and all the carriages career off the lines. It was a cold-blooded business, and a single plane could destroy the lives of hundreds of men, with a well-placed bomb or a long burst of machine-gun fire. Shooting down planes was far better. Each man had a chance, not like the poor bastards trapped inside a train carriage or a cattle car. Eddie couldn't stomach this kind of boasting.

Eddie checked his watch. An hour had passed. Clearly the Huns were not sending any of their men up this autumnal morning. He felt his chances ebbing away. Four Huns. It wasn't enough. Then he remembered the attack on Aulnois and took a quick look at his map. The village was a couple of kilometres away from the town of Saint-Libert and just south of a dense forest. He was sure

110

he had flown over that earlier. It would be easy enough to spot, even on a day like this.

He dived away from the blue vista back through the clouds and into the gloom of a dismal November day. Eddie had a good sense of place and direction and quickly spotted the forest and the church tower close by. He looked at his watch. 09.55. The attack was due at any moment.

A short burst of artillery fire blossomed on the ground beneath him, and he wondered about the wisdom of flying too close to that. What an ignominious end – to be hit by your own artillery on the last day of the war. Plenty of pilots he knew had been shot down by their own side in the previous few months.

The bombardment around the village had stopped now and Eddie could see tiny ant-like figures emerging from an embankment to the west. He swerved down, determined to come in alongside them, and when he discovered where the Germans were entrenched, he would fly in low and drop his eggs. He smirked at the term – another British colloquialism his squadron had picked up.

He put his Camel into a steep dive, and felt the familiar surge of excitement that came with the manoeuvre. His speedometer was touching two hundred miles per hour. A Camel could barely make one hundred twenty five in level flight, so diving like this was as fast as anyone could go. It was amazing. At this speed you could get from New York to Boston in an hour . . . it was even faster than a train.

Eddie levelled off behind the first wave of American soldiers, searching the horizon for any sign of the enemy. He was surprised to hear his engine stutter, and was startled to see a trail of black smoke emerge from the left-hand exhaust vents. Had his own soldiers been firing at him?

Whatever had caused that black smoke had come and gone. Maybe it was a faulty fuel mix, a misfiring valve – it could be lots of things. The engine roared on without interruption – no hint of distress in its insistent thrum, and the stick still felt responsive in his hand. The Camel was flying fine; he should just press on. He felt lucky. Maybe there would be a Hun plane up here for him after all, and maybe he would bag his fifth yet.

But there was still the attack below to attend to. His CO was going to wonder what the hell he was doing up here this morning. The troop-support role would give him an excuse even if it was directly against the regulations to take off like that. Eddie wasn't that worried about the CO – especially if the war really was going to end. He could imagine the fuss the New York papers would kick up if he was court-martialled: *Gutsy Flyboy Cashiered for Fighting Hun.*

Checking around in case there were any other aircraft close by, he was disappointed to find himself still alone in the sky and dived down towards the German lines.

CHAPTER 13

9.45 a.m.

Axel Meyer had grown tired of squinting into the dull horizon. He was sure the Americans would be coming sometime that morning, but they were taking their time about it. His new friend Erich told him that he'd heard the Yanks usually attacked at first light. Well, it was long past that. Then shells began to fall in front of him, far enough away to watch them blossom and dissolve without feeling in immediate danger. He nudged Erich and realised he was fast asleep again. So far he had been lucky, but he was sure that soon the *Feldwebel* would find out. And he was equally sure he'd cut Erich's ears off. 'Hey, look out, we've got shells coming in,' he said.

Erich jolted awake and peered over the crenulated wall of the church tower. A blinding flash erupted fifty metres in front of them, and a hot piece of shrapnel shot through the air, rapping sharply on the oversized helmet that sat uncomfortably on Erich's head. *'Jesus,'* he exclaimed, examining the dent. 'That could have gone straight through.'

'Put it back on, you *Dummkopf*,' said Axel.

Two more shells fell around the first crater. 'They're getting our range,' said Axel. He sounded half excited and half terrified. Their tower was such an obvious target for artillery.

'*Feldwebel*,' he shouted between explosions, 'can we come down? The shells are coming closer.'

The *Feldwebel* unleashed a torrent of curses. They were so colourful some of the other soldiers even sniggered. Axel felt a bright red blush flush across his cheeks.

'The *Schwein*,' said Erich. 'He's sent us up here because we're expendable. He doesn't mind us getting killed, as long as we tell him what we can see first.' He grabbed his rifle and pack. 'I'm going down.'

Axel grabbed his arm. 'Don't be stupid, Erich. They'll shoot you. Cowardice in the face of the enemy. Look. You stay here, we might get killed . . .' Another shell exploded close enough to drown the words in Axel's mouth. Soil, roots, stones and hot metal fragments rained down on them like a torrential downpour. Axel's mouth filled with the taste of earth. He reached for his water bottle to rinse it away. 'Go down there, you're dead for sure.'

Erich saw sense. He sat down, his back to the parapet.

'You know what I heard,' he said. 'Last night in the barn one of the older soldiers said these Americans we're expecting to attack us, they're the 370th Regiment. The 370th! I don't like the sound of that. Where are the other 369 regiments? Are they in France too? That's a hell of a lot of men.'

Axel nodded but said nothing. He had a horrible sinking feeling about the Americans. He hoped the *Feldwebel* was right about them being soft.

His stomach lurched and gurgled. He would give anything for a fried egg and a big hunk of bread. Erich heard and laughed. 'I'm starving too. I wonder if these Americans are as hungry as we are.'

Both of them knew in their hearts they wouldn't be. America was the land of plenty. They had all read about it before the war, and watched the newsreels in picture houses: skyscrapers; endless fields of corn and cattle; those great factories churning out everything from motor cars to refrigerators . . .

He thought about everything they had all been asked to give in the hope of a German victory. First it had been their pots and pans. Then iron railings and door handles. Only last year the church bells at Wansdorf were melted down for vital war materials.

He knew it wasn't patriotic but Axel felt exasperated with his rulers. First the farm labourers had gone to fight. Then most of the horses had been taken. Then the fertiliser to make explosives. How could the farmers feed people on what they had left? Now the whole nation was starving. He was sure that was why his mother had died. She had been working on a steam-powered threshing machine. Axel didn't like to think about what happened. Something, her hair, her clothes, had caught in the drive belt. They wouldn't let him see the body. Herr Meyer was convinced his wife was weakened by hunger. Too slow, too lethargic, to take proper precautions around that infernal machine . . .

'Meyer, Becker,' the *Feldwebel*'s voice barked up to them. 'Report.'

The two boys cautiously peered over the stonework to scan the horizon. The sky was musty and clouded from the shelling, dirt particles still suspended in the air. They could still taste them. 'Look, two hundred metres away – just over the brow of the hill . . .' said Axel.

'There's hundreds of the *Schwein* heading straight for us.' Erich couldn't keep the fear from his voice. 'They're coming. Hundreds of them, two hundred metres.'

The *Feldwebel* called out, 'Prepare to fire. Await my command,' in a cold hard voice. His lack of nervousness steadied the men. High in their tower, Axel and Erich heard twenty rifle bolts crack back in a rapid rattle. 'The shelling has stopped,' said Erich.

An insistent buzzing reached their ears a second later. They both peered over the top of the tower.

'Look, a fighter plane. Heading straight for us,' yelled Axel.

He cracked back his rifle bolt and took careful aim at the nose of the plane. It was flying so low he wondered whether it would crash into the tower.

The roar of the engine almost blotted out everything else now. There was the snap of rifle fire from below, and the rattle of a machine gun. The *Feldwebel* was yelling that they should conserve their ammunition for the attacking Yanks, not waste it on a lucky shot at the plane. But no one heard him.

Axel's finger tightened over the trigger. He felt its coldness, damp in the chill autumn morning. This was his first shot of the war. He aimed right at the central hub of the propeller and squeezed the trigger.

Eddie Hertz was reaching for the lever to drop his bombs. These aerial attacks were always a complicated business. Keep your eye on the horizon, watch out for enemy ground fire, make sure you weren't jumped from above by a Hun fighter, choose your targets. Were you high enough to escape your own bomb blast? All of this, every second, you had to concentrate. His right hand found the lever. That tower. There were bound to be soldiers in it – probably a machine-gun nest. He'd take it out. He knew it was a medieval building – had stood there for six hundred years – but this country was full of churches like that, and sparing this one from the war was not worth the American lives he might save by destroying it. He pulled back the stick, certain he had enough distance to climb over the tower, and lifted the bomb release lever.

Free of its two twenty-five-pound bombs, the Camel immediately felt lighter in the air, but no sooner had Eddie began his evasive manoeuvre than the aircraft jolted in his hand. Something had hit the engine. He was absolutely sure of it this time. He could feel the craft struggle in the air, and already he was losing what little altitude he had. The bombs exploded almost simultaneously beneath him. Hot shrapnel peppered the plane.

Axel Meyer watched in amazement as a thin streak of black smoke began to pour from the climbing aircraft. He was so distracted he did not even see the two silver shapes fall from beneath its wings. Two great clouds of earth exploded behind the church and again he and Erich were showered with earth. The pilot had misjudged his drop, but Axel wasn't thinking about that.

He laughed out loud. His first shot of the war and he had hit an American fighter plane. No one would believe him. He clapped Erich on the back. 'Crack shot!' he yelled. Erich slumped forward. Axel shook him. His helmet fell off. A gaping wound was oozing bone and brain from the back of his head. Erich's eyes were open but he saw nothing. A piece of metal from the bombs must have caught him. Axel leaped to the other side of the tower and looked over. Five of his platoon were lying dead or contorted in agony. He searched the sky for the enemy plane and saw it desperately trying to maintain an even flight, with thick black smoke now pouring from its engine. Flickers of flame played around the exhaust vents too. 'Burn in hell, *Drecksau*,' shouted Axel. If that pilot ever got out of his machine, Axel was going to hunt him down and skewer him with his bayonet. Then he heard the *Feldwebel*'s order: 'Select your targets. Wait for my order to fire.' For a moment he had forgotten the American soldiers were coming too.

*   *   *

120

A few seconds after the explosion Eddie Hertz felt his legs begin to burn with a terrible sharp pain. He looked down to see his leather flying boots peppered with perforations, and blood oozing out of the holes. That wouldn't kill him, at least not yet, but he dreaded to think what would happen when he hit the ground. The black smoke, which made seeing where he was going almost impossible, began to choke him. The words of that British song spun through his head:

> *Take the cylinder out of my kidneys*
> *The connecting rod out of my brain . . .*

He fought back a sudden urge to vomit. Maybe it was shock from his wounds. He felt slippery with sweat but chilled to the marrow. Eddie tried to turn his machine around, so he would crash close to, or even behind, the Allied lines. But halfway through his turn the Camel's rotary engine coughed and spluttered to a juddering halt. In the sudden silence, he could hear shouting and firing from close by. His plane dropped towards the ground.

Eddie was lucky. When his engine cut out, he was already flying beneath tree level. He tried to keep the plane level, but the ground was uneven and there were even some fresh shell holes ahead. The aircraft hit the field with a splintering crash and Eddie was jolted brutally in his cockpit as the Camel's flimsy undercarriage collapsed beneath him. He covered his head with his hands and waited for the grinding, screeching, splintering noise to stop. Eddie didn't see his life flash before him, although everything did seem to be happening in slow motion. Instead, he kept thinking, *Is this it? When is that cylinder going to lodge in my brain? How much is it going to hurt?* He even had time to consider whether to peer over his guns to see if the Camel was heading straight into a sturdy obstacle like a house or a big tree, but he decided he would rather not know. All at once his aircraft was thrown into the air, as it hit a dip in the field and flipped over on to its front. As the plane juddered to a halt, Eddie lost consciousness.

The remaining men of Axel's platoon turned their fire on the aircraft that had killed so many of their comrades. Bullets poured into the shattered canvas fuselage. The *Feldwebel* ordered his men to concentrate their attention on the advancing Americans. Even if they hadn't killed the pilot, the fire that had caught in the engine surely would.

Some of the German bullets had hit home. Eddie Hertz was jolted from unconsciousness by a sharp stab of pain in his right thigh. He could taste the smoke from his blazing engine in his throat and sensed bullets piercing the length of his shattered craft. He also realised he was hanging upside down by his harness. Fortunately the Camel's upper wing had held firm in the crash; otherwise he would have been decapitated.

Instinctively he punched the circular release on his harness and dropped like a stone. He only fell a couple of feet, but he felt weak with pain and nausea as his body landed clumsily on the ground. Seeing him fall attracted the attention of the Germans again and shots began to churn up the earth around him. Eddie saw he had crashed a few yards away from a large shell hole and began to crawl towards it with all his remaining strength.

As he dragged himself over the lip of the crater, a machine gun began its sweep and a bullet caught his right bootheel just as he flipped into the dirt interior. This time Eddie had been lucky.

Axel Meyer had seen Eddie's miraculous escape. When the American soldiers had been repulsed, he was going to go into that crater and finish him off. But first they had to stop the incoming attack. He leaned over the tower ramparts and fired several rounds. He hadn't a clue if he'd hit anyone. He couldn't get out of the habit of clos-ing his eyes whenever he fired and the rifle butt kicked hard into his shoulder.

The soldiers were near enough now to tell the men from the officers. Down below, the *Feldwebel* was order-ing them to shoot the ones with the leather straps across their tunics, who were carrying pistols.

There were a great number of soldiers coming towards him and Axel wondered whether he ought to stop firing from up there in the tower. Stop drawing attention to himself. These Americans were taking heavy casualties as they advanced, and he could not believe they would be happy to accept the surrender of the men who had just been killing them. He was sure there was going to be a massacre. This was how his life would end. At the point of an American bayonet. They were just fifty metres away now. He decided to keep his head down. Stay up there and hope they'd all forget about him.

Over in the crater, Eddie Hertz heard voices near by – American voices!

'Hey, fellas,' he yelled. 'Come help me out.'

Two helmeted heads appeared over the brim of the crater. Doughboys. One of them began to negotiate his way down the side of the crater. Then Eddie heard a harsh voice. 'C'mon, you sons of bitches.'

The soldier shouted, 'We'll be back!' His face was flushed with excitement. Eddie thought he looked like he was having the time of his life.

Back in the tower Axel heard the command he was dreading. 'Meyer, Becker, come down to the trench here.' Axel was seized by panic. Should he pretend to be dead? But something compelled him to obey, and he ran two at a time down the spiralling stone steps of the tower and joined those of his comrades who were still alive.

High above the crack and rattle of rifle and machine-gun fire, Axel could hear the now familiar whistle of incoming shells. Surely the Americans would not be firing on them if their own men were so close to their lines? But the shells were coming from a German artillery battery close behind them. The first salvo devastated the row of advancing Americans. They crumpled and faltered, and as more shells began to fall they turned and ran.

Axel's squad could not believe their luck. The barrage stopped almost as suddenly as it had begun, and in their excitement some of them began to storm out of their foxholes and ditches and chase after their fleeing foe.

The *Feldwebel* shouted angrily that they should remain at their posts, but caught up in the moment, they ignored him. Axel was one of the few who stayed.

Eddie Hertz had been covered by waves of falling soil and stones. He marvelled at how he escaped that bombardment. Maybe, like lightning, shells never fell in the same spot twice. He dragged himself forward with his elbows, further into the crater. It was against all logic but it made him feel safer. But the further he moved into its centre, the more he found himself pulled down by the wet, crumbling earth. And now the shell fire had stopped and the air began to clear, he could smell something hideous. There was a body close by – a German soldier, by the look of it. He had been there for a while and rats had already eaten away at his face. The teeth were bared in a macabre grin. The skin protruding from the sleeves of his jacket was starting to turn black. Eddie choked at the stench and placed a sleeve over his nose. Breathing through that made him feel momentarily better, but he had to get away from that corpse.

He scrambled further down the crater, not realising that the bottom was filled with thick mud. Eddie turned around in the quagmire – desperate to escape its oozing grasp. He started to climb up again, but his wounded legs began to sink beneath him. The more he moved, the more he sank into the boggy earth. Eddie froze and fought back a mounting despair. He had felt lucky to have escaped his plane. Now he wasn't so sure.

CHAPTER 14

10.00 a.m.

The sniper had shaken them all. Will could see it in their faces. And now they could hear shooting and explosions in the middle distance, somewhere over to the south. That didn't help.

Jim was being extra terse with his commands. He needed to be stern. He sensed the men's fear too. The last thing he wanted was to have them panic and flee like frightened rabbits. Then they could be picked off one by one. Together they could concentrate their fire on any threat.

'I'll carry on at point,' said Jim, continuing to place himself in the most exposed position and putting hope and courage back into his patrol. 'Now keep those ears flapping and no unnecessary talking. We're going t'make our way back to the platoon. Fritz probably has several snipers in these woods. We'll report back and get the artillery to blow this place to splinters.'

Will felt a huge sense of relief when Jim announced they were going. He was desperate to be away from this gloomy forest. He was convinced that hostile eyes were watching him, or worse, even at that moment, someone had him in the cross hairs of a telescopic sight. He had to force himself to stop wondering if these were the last thoughts he would ever have.

He tried to cheer himself up. There were still seven of them left. That gave Will a sense of security.

As they trudged back, steady rain trickled down through the trees to add to their misery. The forest was dark at the best of times. Now it was almost like patrolling at dusk. Jim held up his hand, bringing them all to a halt. He beckoned Will forward and pointed to a black shape in the undergrowth close to the path, indicating he should have a look. It looked like the sole of a boot.

Will moved forward cautiously, then flinched at the sight before him. Two skeletons, bones bleached by the elements, were lying on their backs close to each other. Both still had their army boots on their feet, but there was no evidence of any other clothing or weapons. Will beckoned the others to come and look. 'Watch out for booby traps,' whispered Jim to them all as they gathered round the macabre spectacle.

'Maybe they were sunbathing,' sniggered one of the men.

'Glad someone finds it funny,' said Jim brusquely. The soldier's smirk vanished in an instant.

'They were the boots they gave out to soldiers in 1914 – the original British Expeditionary Force,' said Jim. 'I remember them. Look at the stitching. These fellas were killed at the start of the war – probably retreating back from Mons in the late summer.

'Jesus Christ!' he said in despair, looking up to the sky. He turned his back on his men as he tried to stop his face crumpling up. Will felt for him but didn't dare put a consoling arm on his shoulder. He could see the other men looking uncomfortable. No one liked to see their sergeant so vulnerable. He was a tough bastard, and if he started to go, then what chance had the rest of them?

Jim took a few deep breaths, until he could be sure his voice was steady. Then he said, 'It's taken us all this time, and all these blessed dead soldiers, to get back to where we were over four years ago. Don't know who was luckier – them or us that's had to carry on fighting . . .'

He turned abruptly. 'Come on, let's get the bloody hell out of here.'

They began to walk back west. Jim had his compass out and that gave them a rough sense of the direction they needed to be going in. No one said a word, each of them completely wrapped up in scanning the gloom for movements. But it was difficult to tell whether a shifting branch was caused by a sniper or the wind.

Even though they were tired, the men picked up speed. They were all anxious to get out of the forest with no further casualties. After fifteen minutes, Jim raised an arm to signal a halt. 'Right, two minutes' rest,' he whispered, 'and then Cowell can take point.'

Cowell nodded. They set off without a word when Jim got up. The rain had stopped at least, but the sky above, as far as they could see through the canopy of leaves and branches, was still leaden.

Will was next in line, with Cowell at least five yards ahead. It was standard patrol procedure. You kept a good distance to make it more difficult for a sniper with a quick trigger finger to pick off a group of men in a few seconds, or to prevent a sudden artillery or mortar shell wiping out the whole patrol.

There were more bodies ahead of them. Five German soldiers – very recently killed, by the look of them. The trees around them were scarred and tattered from shell blast. It was not difficult to see what had happened here.

'They were probably after us too,' whispered Jim. 'No

sign of 'em when we came this way before. Wonder if there are any more German patrols?'

Will shook his head and tried to control the terrible anxiety that lurked in his gut. He just wanted to run as fast as he could out of the forest.

As they hurried past, Will looked at the bodies, with their weapons and supplies scattered around them. Two were lying separate from the others. Three had been caught in a tight bunch – maybe they were leaning in to light a cigarette from a single match – maybe they had been having a whispered conversation. Now they lay tangled together. Most were untouched, save for bleeding around the ears or nose. They had yet to take on the stench of death. One, a young soldier close to Will's age, had a letter poking out the top of his trouser pocket.

Will hated seeing the personal belongings of dead men. The wristwatch, the shaving kit, the comb, the penknife, the mess tin and spoon and fork, and especially the letters from home. These things all had a terrible intimacy – once of great value to their dead owner, now worthless.

As Jim's patrol hurried on, something stirred in the pile of bodies. The man had heard them coming and, in his haste to hide, had realised the safest spot was in among these dead soldiers. He wondered where his fellow sniper Hoffmayer was, and whether he had managed to add to his total today. They had set off at first light this morning, and had bet a bottle of schnapps on who would claim the most kills by sunset. He'd already caught some fool out in the open, shouting to draw attention to himself. That was too easy. He wondered if Hoffmayer had had similar luck.

Moving with extreme care, he slowly placed his rifle to his shoulder and peered at the back of the last man in the line. He needed to wait a moment or two more. The further away they were, the less they would be able to tell where the shot came from. He also hoped there might be further shell fire from somewhere, to hide the sound of his rifle. He breathed deeply and slowly, keeping his eye on his target and his finger by the trigger. Not too close though. Like many snipers he had filed down the levers on the firing mechanism of his Mauser, to make the trigger more responsive. It was a mixed blessing. An unintended shot could easily give him away.

The path ahead of Jim's patrol veered off to the north, but they could see it was close to another path heading in the direction they needed to go. Cowell took a short cut through the low undergrowth and all at once he disappeared in a white flash of earth and flame.

Seeing the flash and the flying debris, the sniper's finger touched his trigger. He hit his target in the back of the neck. He could not have done a better job if he'd standing right behind him with a pistol.

Will, standing nearest to Cowell, was knocked off his feet. His head buzzed from the noise of the explosion, but he could not feel any other sort of injury. How he had escaped he did not really understand. When he looked at Cowell again, he was lying on his side with a tattered leg oozing blood and a horrible white stump of bone above where his left foot should be.

'Hold back,' said Jim urgently. He moved cautiously forward. 'That were a mine, weren't it?' he asked his men. 'I didn't hear a shell coming in. Stick to the path. Keep your eyes ahead – and watch where you're putting your feet.'

Will could see his brother talking but he couldn't hear him. There was just a whistle in his head. It didn't hurt or anything, but it made him feel trapped, not being able to hear anything.

The sniper cursed. The men in the patrol were now dispersed. His line of fire was no longer clear, but at least they hadn't noticed another of their men was missing. He kept watching them flit between the trees.

Wait. That's what snipers did. His moment would come again.

Sergeant Franklin edged over to Cowell. 'He's still breathing. Must have knocked him unconscious.'

Cowell stirred, then began to moan. Then he started to scream. He looked down at his injury. 'My leg. The bastards, they've blown off my bloody leg.'

Jim propped him up. 'It's just your foot, Cowell. The rest of you is all right. Try not to make a noise.' He took a flask from his backpack. 'Drink some of this rum.'

Cowell gulped it down until he choked. 'Jesus it hurts,' he said, gritting his teeth. He was pale now, his eyes slipping in and out of focus.

Jim took some bandages from his pack and began to improvise a rough tourniquet. 'Stay with us, Cowell,' he said. Then he turned to the biggest man in the squad. 'Bradshaw, will you run ahead with him, get him to a field station as quick as you can?'

It was a request rather than an order. But Bradshaw didn't need a second bidding. Before the war he had worked down the mines and he could pick a man up as easily as he could heft a sack of coal. He put a hand on Cowell's shoulder and said, 'Don't you worry, mate, I'll get you back,' then hauled him up. Cowell flinched as his injured leg brushed against his comrade.

Bradshaw hurried off ahead, Cowell's body bent over his shoulder, and the others marvelled at his strength.

Will watched them go. He wanted to get out of this forest more than anything else he had done in his life. His hearing was coming back in little bursts. Sometimes clear, sometimes just a whistle.

There was a sudden *crack*, like a twig being snapped, and all of them turned to look at Bradshaw and Cowell. The big man stumbled and lurched forward, stopped in his tracks. He and Cowell fell to the ground in an instant. Neither of them moved. All of the patrol threw themselves down. Then Ogden stood up to get a better view. Jim immediately signalled for him to get down. Will could see a small bloody circle right in the centre of Cowell's back. It was getting bigger by the second.

'The clever bastard,' Will heard Jim say to no one in particular. 'Got them both with a single shot.'

'What do we do now, Sarge?' said Hosking.

'We wait,' said Jim. 'Stay here till dark if we have to. Keep looking around. But make your movements really slowly.'

'Let's hope he's not up in one of these trees, and can see us on the ground,' said Hosking. He sounded terrified, and Will felt his own fear in the pit of his stomach.

But they were covered pretty well, kneeling in deep foliage in a dip in the ground. They should be hidden.

Jim called quietly, 'Weale, where are you, man?' He sounded on edge – as near to frightened as Will had ever heard him. Will suddenly realised Weale had not been among them since Cowell had caught the mine.

'I haven't seen him, just now,' said Ogden in a terrified whisper.

Will raised his head to take a look around and see if he could spot his comrade. A shot immediately rang out, hitting the side of his helmet in such a way that it knocked it off his head. In that one instant all four of them were seized with a blind urge to run. They scattered, each one in any direction his legs would carry him, praying that he could run fast enough to outwit the hidden enemy there in the forest.

CHAPTER 15

10.15 a.m.

Axel counted the remaining men from his unit. There were fifteen of them left. Some of those who had chased the retreating Americans were returning. They looked fearful, wondering what punishment their bravado would earn them. A few wounded men were having their injuries attended to. Some still thrashed and whimpered in their agony, but the screaming had mercifully ceased.

The calm that had descended seemed unreal. Axel felt like he was in a dream. Everything, even on this dim, drab day, seemed pin sharp. His breath in the cold air, raindrops on grass, pools of water glistening in the mud, the grey clouds, the rise and fall of his chest as he breathed. He was still alive. He had survived his first combat unscathed. He thought he would feel more upset or shaken by what had happened. Maybe that would come later.

The *Feldwebel* ignored the men who had come back, which surprised Axel, who had expected him to berate them with his usual ferocity. Maybe he felt they had shown the correct fighting spirit. Now he was sitting in a dip in the ground, cleaning his rifle, a smouldering clay pipe clamped firmly in his mouth. Even sitting down he still seemed like an enormous physical presence. Axel approached him with trepidation. '*Feldwebel*, my comrade Becker has been killed by a bomb. I ask permission to inspect the crashed aircraft and ensure the pilot is dead.'

The *Feldwebel* nodded abruptly. 'Return shortly,' he said.

Axel withdrew his bayonet from its sheath and fixed it to the mount on his Mauser rifle. It had repelled him when he was first issued with it. On the underside of the pointed blade were serrations. 'What is this for?' he had asked the drill sergeant, expecting it to be some bloody form of torture. 'It's a saw, you *Dummkopf*,' the man had replied. 'What do you think?' Now that bayonet looked entirely fit for its gruesome purpose.

He wriggled out of his field pack and ran over the freshly churned ground. The crashed fighter plane was still burning fiercely and thick black smoke was rising into the grey sky. He could feel the heat of it as he approached.

As he reached the edge, he dropped to the ground and cautiously peered over. There was a terrible stink coming from inside the crater. He saw the grinning corpse and recoiled in revulsion. Then he saw the American airman at the bottom of the crater. He hadn't spotted him yet.

Axel took a deep breath and steeled himself for what he was about to do. He would run straight towards the pilot and skewer him with his bayonet. He deserved no less. He tensed and hurled himself over the edge – he would be upon his enemy in a matter of seconds and then it would be all over. He ran at full pelt, his rifle raised and ready to strike.

Only when he was almost upon the pilot did he realise he was staring straight into the barrel of his revolver. Instinctively he froze in his tracks. Did he have a bullet in the chamber of his rifle? He couldn't remember. He certainly wouldn't be able to cock his rifle and fire off a round before the airman shot him in the face.

They stared at each other for a few seconds, frozen in time – Axel with his rifle raised and his bayonet a few inches away from Eddie's face. Eddie, his arm out, was holding a revolver pointing straight at Axel.

Axel became aware again of his breathing and his heart beating painfully hard in his chest. But strangest of all was how calm he felt. Why had the American not shot him when he had charged towards him? What were they going to do next?

The pilot, it seemed, had the advantage, but Axel noticed how the revolver was shaking in his hand. Its weight seemed too much for him and Axel realised he must be badly wounded. Should he wait to see what happened next, or should he press home his attack? He searched his opponent's face for a sign. His hand might be shaking, but his eyes seemed clear and well focused. Then he noticed his face. He looked strangely familiar. The man had the sort of ruddy colouring often seen in the region he came from. And he wasn't really a man – he was only a year or two older than Axel.

'Just put the rifle down and catch your breath,' said the pilot, speaking German with a Berlin accent.

'You're German,' blurted out Axel. 'Why are you fighting for them?'

'Don't be a *Dummkopf*,' said the pilot. 'Put down your rifle or I'm going to have to kill you. *I* don't want to die on the last day of the war, and I don't want *you* to have to either.'

Axel was reeling. This airman spoke German like a native. And, he knew, he could easily have shot him just now. He began to shake a little himself. His anger was dissolving and, much to his embarrassment, he realised he was having to fight back tears.

'What's your name, son?' said Eddie. He had realised this boy was his only chance out of this pool of mud. He needed to win him over quickly, before he sank further.

'Axel,' said the boy warily. 'Why are you talking to me like this? Are you a traitor? Have you changed sides?'

Eddie laughed. 'Look, my parents moved over to the United States forty years ago. I was born there. We speak German at home, and English everywhere else. I'm as American as those soldiers who were attacking you just now.'

Axel noticed the airman had a woman's scarf poking out from the top of his flying jacket. Then another thing he'd just heard hit him like a flash of lightning. He blinked in confusion. 'What did you say . . . the last day of the war?' he blurted.

Eddie laughed again – this time in disbelief. 'What! They haven't told you?'

Axel felt exasperated. 'Well, they didn't tell your soldiers attacking just now, did they! They didn't tell your artillery men . . .' He could feel his anger boiling up and raised his rifle. 'And if you knew the war was ending today, what the hell were you doing coming over here in your flying machine and killing all my comrades?'

Eddie's eyes flashed with anger too. He levelled his revolver at Axel's head again. 'Stay where you are and calm yourself.'

Axel froze.

'Our top brass . . .' said Eddie, then he faltered. All of a sudden he was having to find the strength to talk. 'Got reputations to make. Gonna keep us fighting right to the eleventh hour . . . Then it's all over, *Kamerad* . . . You stay here with me and wait.' He glanced very rapidly at his watch and his eyes returned to Axel. 'Not long . . . then we can both go home to our mothers.'

Eddie felt guilty, making this speech. After all, he too had set out at the break of day to add a final notch to his belt. All at once he realised he was no better than any of the rest of the glory hunters – hoping to impress the other pilots by taking the life of another man.

'I came out to help our boys,' he lied to Axel and to himself. 'If our boys are attacking, then it's my job to help them.'

Axel felt confused. This pilot he had been so intent on killing was only doing his duty – like they all were. And the man could have killed him easily enough. Axel extended an arm, reaching further down to make contact.

But the pilot warned him away. 'Don't come any closer. I'm stuck in the mud here. You need to get something, a rope and plank, a belt, to pull me out.'

Eddie wondered whether he had told this boy too much. He was at his mercy. What would he do if the boy refused to help? Threaten to shoot him?

Axel decided what to do in an instant. Otto had told him stories about the trenches. How men had fought like devils but shared cigarettes or water bottles with the enemy after the fighting. The thing that haunted him most, said his brother, was the Tommy he had killed after he had surrendered. But some other enemy soldiers, just up the line, were still fighting. Grenades were coming over. 'Kill him,' snapped Otto's lieutenant, and Otto just lunged in with his bayonet. 'He looked so surprised, and then he screamed and called for his mother. I can still hear him now. If you have to fight, be careful what you do. You'll have to live with it for the rest of your life.'

So Axel Meyer undid the belt around his trousers and tossed it towards Eddie Hertz. He noticed Eddie's eyes went out of focus, and there was sweat on his brow, even though he was up to his thighs in freezing mud . . . Axel knew instinctively he needed first aid. But he couldn't risk taking him back to his own lines. His own comrades would kill him.

'Hey, Axel, keep your mind on the job,' the pilot was telling him.

Axel began to pull hard on the belt, but Eddie kept losing his grip. He was stuck pretty thoroughly here. 'Wrap it round your hand,' said Axel. 'I'll lean forward some more.'

Eddie did, and Axel pulled with all his strength. But instead of drawing Eddie out, he lurched forward himself and his feet sank deep into the muddy water. In a panic he tried to lift a leg. He was stuck too.

'*Jesus,*' he said in despair. He waited a moment, then tried to lift his left leg again. It was stuck in the mud like it was held there by a giant magnet. 'Hold steady, Axel,' said the pilot. 'We wait. Wait until the firing stops, wait until we hear some cheering, and some church bells, then we start shouting our heads off.'

For a few moments neither said anything. Axel was wondering what sort of hellish mess he had got himself into. Then shells began to fall again, close to their own crater. The first few were far enough away to just hear, but then a brace began to fall near enough for them to hear the scream as they came in. Soil fell around them, and the air was snatched from their lungs. Their ears began to whistle with the noise, then something screamed in right close to them. 'Dear God,' said Eddie in English. There

145

was a great thump right next to them, and earth splattered up. Axel looked around. Why weren't they dead? A small crater had appeared in front of them, not two metres away. They could see the hole the shell had made as it plunged into the damp earth.

They both stared at it, expecting to be blown to pieces at any second. Axel was frozen in terrified expectation. But as nothing happened, the dread he felt gradually began to ebb from his limbs. Instead, he started to shake all over.

'It must be a dud,' he said. Otto had told him about shells that landed close by but didn't explode.

'Either that or a delayed fuse,' said Eddie. 'Let's hope it's not ticking.' He paused and tried to sound more cheerful. 'No. It's a message from God. He wants us to live. Sit tight, Axel. We're going to see the end of this war. You got a girl back home? Well, I've got one here, and I'm not planning on dying on her.'

CHAPTER 16

10.30 a.m.

Will ran until his lungs were bursting, expecting a shot in the head at any second. Did you hear it before it hit you? Did you feel it? Or would you never know? Men he had seen shot through the head sometimes had a look of dull surprise etched on their dead faces. Once, he had been working on a burial detail with the new padre, Reverend Oliver. There was a dead fellow with a surprised look on his face. Oliver had said it was because, at the moment of his death, he had seen an old friend who had come to take him off to heaven. Will tried to hide his annoyance. He was too old for stories like that.

Will could run no further and he collapsed on to a thick patch of vegetation, gulping down great lungfuls of air. His mouth seemed very damp, and when he wiped it he was surprised to find his hand was covered in blood. Then he remembered that when his helmet had been shot from his head it had been knocked down over his face. The rim must have hit his nose, which had bled quite profusely. Inspecting it now, he didn't know whether it was broken or just badly bruised. It hurt like hell when he touched it.

His hearing was still not right either. It was as if someone was closing his ears with their hands, then taking them away again. He lay there, occasionally banging the side of his head to try to stop the whistling and those strange dense blanks when he could hear nothing at all.

He surrendered to the silence and lay on his back, staring up through the treetops to the cloud-covered sky. Will didn't believe any of that nonsense about heaven. How God could put these good-hearted men through such a living hell was beyond his understanding. The new padre said God moved in mysterious ways. Will didn't like the Reverend Oliver. He looked at you like the village vicar used to look at the poorer boys when they put their grubby fingers in the biscuit tray at the school fête. Will preferred the padre they had had before. But, oddly, he was the reason Will no longer believed in God.

The Reverend Charles Clare was a toff. He'd been to Oxford University. But he would come right down to the firing line to mingle with the men, helping the slower ones with their letters. His wife made beautiful fruitcake, and when a package came over, he'd share it with them all. And he'd put a word in for old Pierce, the one who had been shaking so bad he couldn't hold his rifle. The one the CO wanted to shoot for cowardice.

One morning the reverend announced his wife had just had twins. They were his first kids. One of the blokes knitted a couple of pairs of socks for the babies and went off to find him. Will had been surprised to discover quite a few of the men knitted on the front line. The man came back white as a sheet, still holding on to those little blue socks. 'He's in the latrine,' he said. 'Trousers round his ankles, top of his head missing. Stray bit of shell burst must have had him.' Then he turned round and threw up. None of the men could understand how God could do that to one of his own.

After that, Will was convinced he lived in a rudderless world and only blind luck was going to save him. That didn't stop him praying though – when they were under heavy fire or the shells were falling.

Now, as he lay on the edge of the forest, Will's breathing slowly returned to normal. His heart stopped thumping in his chest and he began to feel a creeping sense of fear – not for the sniper, wherever he was. He had missed him for now. But Will had run away. He examined his conscience. Had they all run, or was it just him? In his mind's eye, he replayed the scene. The shot that set him off had glanced off his helmet, and they had all run off, at least that's what he remembered. But where were the others now? He daren't call out for fear of drawing the attention of the sniper. He was even reluctant to stand up and look around in case he was spotted. What was he going to do? If he stayed there, alone in his sheltered hiding place, was he deserting? Was he showing cowardice in the face of the enemy? You could be shot for that. What should he do?

They had shot a boy just like him in early September. Jim said they had done it to encourage the others. Damn right it had. It had certainly worked on Will.

Peering through the foliage, Will realised he was close to the very edge of the forest. A short distance away he could see the trees abruptly end and could just make out a wide, flat field ahead.

The outside world was intruding. In the distance he could hear firing and shell bursts. Will lay there for a few more minutes, trying to make up his mind what to do. Eventually, he decided he had to move on. He began to crawl forward to the edge of the forest and peered anxiously out.

Ahead lay flat ground, obviously the scene of a recent battle. There were fresh craters and the smell of explosives and wet earth still hung in the air, along with acrid smoke from the blazing fuselage of a plane. He wondered if that was the one he had seen flying low over the forest earlier that morning. For now he could not see any other soldiers, but he was beginning to feel an overwhelming urge to get out of the forest. The landscape ahead of him was unfamiliar. There was nothing he remembered from entering the forest in the early-morning light. Perhaps this was on the other side? He had completely lost any sense of direction.

He crawled away from the shadow of the trees and into the churned-up ground before him. It was a laborious process, crawling forward like that, but Will didn't want to stand up. A lone soldier in a field was just asking to be picked off by an enemy soldier – or even a careless one from his own side. It was a pity he no longer had his helmet. That would have made it obvious who he was.

Close to the burning plane he could see a deep crater. Beyond that was a small village. There was a church tower, a manor house and a few buildings. Will decided he would head for that. See what he might find.

It took him ten minutes to reach the crater. He peered cautiously over the lip, then froze in horror. There were two figures down at the bottom, observing him with fearful expressions on their faces. Then an awful stench hit him. Something else was in there – a dead man at the other side of the crater.

One of the two who were still alive was a German soldier. It was at this moment Will realised, with a shiver that went all down his body, he no longer had his rifle. He could not remember where he had left it – probably in the forest when his helmet had been shot off, or close to the edge of the wood before he had crawled out here. There would be hell to pay for that. Throwing away your weapon was definitely a court-martial charge. How he had not noticed until now, he could not understand.

So far he had escaped the horrors of the day and his every instinct told him to flee. But then the German soldier called up, '*Hilfe!*' and held out his hand. He sounded timid and desperate. Will looked again. He was barely older than him.

The other fellow down there was more difficult to place. The man's head was slumped forward, but then he jerked it up, as if waking from a nap. He wore the leather helmet and goggles of an airman. It must have been him in that Yank aeroplane.

Will realised at once the two of them were stuck in the mud that oozed thick and black at the bottom of the crater. He didn't care that one of them was German.

He couldn't leave them to sink and drown, like poor Stan.

He slipped down the crater's side, but the closer he got the more he could feel he was sinking into the soggy earth. 'Wait,' he called. 'I'll come back in a minute.'

He heard a voice call after him. 'Hey, pal . . .' It sounded weak but panicky, someone who was using their last reserves of strength to beg for help. 'Don't go. Stay and help us. Don't go like the other guys . . .'

Will turned around again. 'I need a stick – a branch – something to reach you with,' he said. 'I promise I'll be back as soon as I can.' He began to scramble up again.

A shot rang out, burying itself into the wet earth just next to him. Will froze and turned. The one in the flying jacket held a pistol in his outstretched arms.

'You gotta stay and help us,' he pleaded. He sounded desperately weary. Will shouted angrily, 'Why did you shoot at me? We're on the same side, aren't we?'

'Look, if I stay stuck here much longer I'm gonna die,' said the pilot. 'I already had a bunch of my own soldiers come down and then run off before they could get me out.'

Will crept gingerly down the side of the crater, as near to the two of them as he could without getting sucked into the mud. The German boy stared at him with something approaching revulsion.

The pilot was still pointing his pistol at him. Will tried to sound as reasonable as he could. 'Please don't do that. I need to get something to help you. I don't want to get sucked into the mud too.' As he spoke, he felt dried blood crack on his face.

'What the hell happened to you?' said the pilot.

Will realised his face must be covered in blood. That was what happened when your nose bled. It looked so much worse than it really was.

'If you let me go, I will come back soon with something to pull you out of here,' he said.

'Swear to me you'll come back,' said the pilot. He seemed close to panic. 'Don't go dying on us. Don't get killed out there.'

'I will come back, but only if you put your revolver away,' said Will. The pilot gave an embarrassed grin – the nearest Will was going to get to an apology – and put the gun back in his holster.

So Will crawled back across the field to the edge of the forest. He didn't care if one of them was a German, he was determined to get those two out. Sinking into mud to freeze to death, or even worse, to drown. It was the stuff of nightmares. He reached the dense line of trees, grateful that no one had taken a shot at him. It had gone quiet, and only in the distance could he hear the occasional shell or rifle shot. He wondered if it was his hearing, but when he clicked his fingers he could hear that perfectly.

On the edge of the forest, just where the trees gave way to the open field, was exactly what he was looking for – a long thin branch, recently fallen from a tree. He picked it up and bashed it on the ground. It seemed sturdy, certainly not rotten or so weak that it would snap if anyone grabbed hold of it.

Will crawled back, still surprised by how quiet this recently churned-up battlefield had become. He heard the occasional chirp and wondered if it was his hearing playing up again. Then he realised what he could hear was birdsong.

Will reached the crater, half expecting to find both of these strangers had gone. But they were still there and the look on their faces when he appeared reassured him that they were not going to do him harm. He slid down the inside again, dragging his branch, and held it out to the German boy.

'Hey, Limey,' said the flyer. 'This kid's OK. Don't worry about him.' His voice seemed stronger. He seemed to have revived, now the prospect of rescue was imminent.

Will noticed a German rifle at the side of the crater.

The boy had obviously put it down there when he went to rescue the pilot. He would keep an eye on him though, make sure he got to the rifle before the German, if there was any funny business.

The flyer had noticed him looking at the weapon. 'Don't worry about him,' he called wearily. 'He's a good kid, I told you. And if he decides not to be, I still got my revolver.'

Will held out the branch to the boy and dug his boots into the mud to steady himself. He could feel his feet sinking as the boy pulled hard, but he came out eventually. '*Danke! Danke!*' the boy said, then, 'Sank yew, *Kamerad!*'

The flyer was more difficult to get out. Both of them pulled on the branch, but the man was too weak to hold on. The German boy had an idea. He took off his leather belt and fastened it to the end of the branch with the buckle, just above a knobbly lump.

Then they both held it over the flyer's head. The pilot grabbed the dangling leather strap, and wrapped it around his wrists. With all three of them straining to get him out, they made progress – and eventually he lurched forward in a great splash of mud and water, and an agonising yelp. They dragged him by the scruff of his flying jacket halfway up the crater.

The relief on the pilot's face was heartening but Will could see how badly wounded he was. Blood mingled with mud all along his lower legs. Will carried a small first-aid kit in a pouch on his belt, but there was no point trying to patch up this Yank until they had the chance to wash those wounds.

Lost in the moment, neither Will nor the American thought to keep an eye on the German boy, and now they were out Will half expected to find himself staring down the barrel of a Mauser. But instead, the boy grabbed him by the sleeve and said something Will did not understand. But he knew it was urgent.

The pilot looked alarmed. 'Oh yeah. There's a shell here, landed about half an hour ago. We don't know whether it's a dud or whether it's on a timed fuse,' he said rapidly. 'I'd quite forgotten about it.'

Will and the other boy grabbed the flyer and hauled him up. As they reached the lip of the crater, they could hear distant cheering. 'What's happening?' Will blurted out.

The flyer turned to the German boy and smiled broadly, his pearly teeth flashing against the mud and oil on his face. 'I told you the war was about to end,' he said in German. Then he turned to Will and said, 'It's all over. Look. Eleven o'clock.' He held out his wristwatch.

It was covered in mud, but he wiped it so Will could see the time. 'We're done. It's all over.'

Will was dumbfounded. He thought he'd be fighting all the way to Berlin – if he lived that long. Then he felt a sudden burst of anger. Why had they sent them in to the wood if they knew the war was about to end? He thought of the men who had been killed on the last morning of the war. What about those snipers? Did they know? He had to know if the Germans knew too. 'Ask him – ask Fritz here if he knew the war was about to end.'

'Hey, steady!' said the pilot angrily. 'He didn't know either. I only found out about nine o'clock this morning.'

With sudden horror Will thought of Jim. He wondered if his brother had been caught by the sniper.

The American interrupted his train of thought by leaning forward and offering Will a hand to shake. 'I'm Pilot Officer Eddie Hertz, American Air Service First Pursuit Group. How do you do?' he said in an affectionate parody of a formal Englishman.

'I'm Will, how do you do?'

'And this here is Axel,' said Eddie. The two boys shook hands stiffly. Will thought it was bizarre, these drawing-room manners, but the whole situation was like a strange dream.

Axel eyed Will warily. He had not forgotten that the

British made a habit of dropping grenades in prisoners' pockets.

'We can all be friends again now,' said Eddie airily. 'The war is over, so play nicely.' Then he collapsed on the ground. 'Can you boys get me to a first-aid post,' he said, first in English and then in German. 'There's a town over that way.'

The ground they were on was slightly raised above the rest of the terrain. They could see a small town a mile or so over to the east.

Axel spoke rapidly to Eddie who nodded weakly. He turned to Will and said, 'Axel thinks it would take an hour to carry me to the town. He doesn't reckon that would do these holes in my leg much good. I guess he has a point. He says there's a German position by the church right behind us. I can get these wounds cleaned up there at least and wait for help.'

Axel didn't know what his soldiers were likely to do to a pilot who had just bombed them, but the war was over. They would have to take that risk.

Will was wary too. Was this a ruse? Could they trust this German boy? They had no choice. The American was deathly white now. Will tried to put Jim out of his thoughts and felt a renewed determination to save this pilot. They would make sure he was comfortable, then

Will would try to find his unit and hope to God his brother had managed to rejoin them too. He wondered why he didn't feel pleased that he was still alive. He had assumed every day would be his last. Perhaps he couldn't quite bring himself to believe it was really over.

CHAPTER 17

11.10 a.m.

The two boys hoisted Eddie's arms over their shoulders and began to hobble towards Axel's line. They tried not to make rapid movements – every jolt through the field seemed to bring the pilot further pain. It seemed strange, unnatural, walking upright in plain view of any enemy snipers. But the war was over now and they could hardly drag the pilot along the ground.

'Wait here,' said Axel, and they put Eddie down. Then Axel ran forward shouting in German. 'He's telling them not to fire, that he has found a wounded man,' Eddie translated for Will. 'He's all right,' he said. 'I told you.'

Axel disappeared from view, but he came back almost immediately.

'Gone,' he shouted. 'They must have withdrawn.'

They would have to go to the town after all. They picked Eddie up and continued past the church where he'd dropped his bombs. The German boy seemed numb with anguish. They could see a few dead bodies. '*Sieh Dir das an*,' – Look at this – said Axel, gesturing towards the fallen soldiers. Will didn't understand but he could hear the anger in his voice. For a second or two he wondered if Axel was going to walk off and leave him alone with Eddie. He wouldn't be able to carry him on his own.

Eddie hung his head – from shame or exhaustion Will couldn't tell. Axel stayed with them, anger still blazing in his eyes.

The road to the town passed along the outer edge of the wood. It was all downhill, which helped. They approached a German command post, with a flag and telephone wires disappearing into a trench and dugout. Axel called out, but there was no reply. It too had been abandoned.

Axel spoke to Eddie, then left him with Will and ran towards it. 'He's going to see if they've left water or first-aid supplies.'

Will panicked. 'Stop,' he shouted. The warning in his voice was enough to make Axel hesitate. Over the last few weeks Will had been through several recently evacuated enemy positions and he knew they were potential death traps for the unwary.

He helped Eddie sit down on a tree stump and was alarmed to see Axel was already climbing down into the trench. 'Wait!' Will screamed, beckoning him back. His gestures must have made sense because Axel came out at once with a puzzled look on his face.

Peering into the dugout trench, Will could see one of the duckboards at the bottom was sticking up a little. It was a trick Jim had warned his men about soon after Will arrived at the Front.

Will took a sandbag from the side of the trench and emptied some of it out so he could pick it up. He beckoned Axel to take cover. Then he tossed it down and threw himself flat on the ground beside him. A second or two later there was an explosion and the side of the trench was peppered with splinters and shrapnel.

Patting Axel on the shoulder he said, 'Watch this.' Will picked up another sandbag and hurled it through the open door of the dugout. Another explosion followed, and the dugout collapsed in on itself.

'*Danke*,' said Axel. For the first time, he gave Will what seemed like a genuine smile.

Will had seen several of his own platoon lost to booby traps in abandoned enemy positions. Any *Pickelhaube* helmet left in an obvious place, or officer's pistol, or bayonet – all tempting souvenirs – were likely to have a wire and a charge attached. Flags on poles were another common one. Arriving at a recently vacated German command post, Will had seen two men blown to pieces when they had hurried over to grab an Imperial German Army flag.

Will ran back to Eddie, beckoning Axel to hurry, and after another twenty minutes of slow, exhausting walking, they reached the outskirts of the town. It too seemed deserted. Palls of smoke rose from several points. The acrid smell of burning buildings mingled with the low stench of sewage and leaking gas from pipes ruptured in the recent bombardment.

'There's bound to be water here, supplies,' whispered Eddie. 'Even if the locals have fled.'

They reached a large square, overlooked by a medieval church at one end and a railway station at the other. There were shops here – windows boarded up – and still no people. The square was full of debris – masses of equipment left behind by a fleeing army – backpacks, field guns, even a wagon full of hay for horses that had also fled.

Will called out, 'Is anyone here? Help! We have an injured man!' His voice echoed around the square.

They looked around. In the distance they could hear two dogs barking at one another. Will hoped they didn't come any closer. Dogs, driven into a frenzy by artillery fire or hunger, were terrifying to deal with. Will had had to shoot one once.

'I need water,' said Eddie weakly.

Will knew those wounds needed washing as soon as possible. The American was heading for a nasty dose of gangrene if he couldn't clean him up.

'Let's put you down on that hay wagon,' said Will. 'Then I'll look for some water.' They carried him across the square and gently laid him down in the hay.

'Tell Fritz here to help me find some water,' said Will to Eddie.

Axel gave him a dirty look. He spoke very little English, but he knew the English called the Germans 'Fritz' or 'the Hun', after the savage barbarian foes of the Romans. Both words were meant as an insult. He cursed himself for leaving his rifle in the shell crater.

Eddie picked up Axel's hostility. He needed these boys to look after him, not start fighting. 'Easy fella,' he said to Will. 'War's over. Why not call him Axel?' The effort exhausted him.

Eddie spoke to Axel and the German boy nodded. He went over to the pile of backpacks abandoned in the square, searching for water bottles. Will looked around, hoping to find a water pump. He was lucky. Close to an empty fountain by the church there was a stirrup pump. Will shouted over, asking Axel to bring a container. Eddie translated for him, although his voice faltered as he tried to speak loud enough for the German boy to hear him.

Axel hurried over with an abandoned bucket and held it under the pump as Will worked the handle. Water dribbled out in a trickle and the bucket took an age to fill. When Axel looked down, his feet were soaking. The bucket was leaking. Will put a hand under the bottom, and they hurried back to Eddie. He seemed to be asleep. He was still breathing at least.

Axel carefully undid the zips on Eddie's flying boots, but the pilot screamed himself conscious when they tried to take them off. Blood had hardened over the shrapnel perforations. Will could see an army blanket among the debris in the square so he ran over to pick it up. He still had his bayonet on his webbing and used it to cut a strip off. The blanket was pretty filthy, but he needed something to use as a sponge. Will dampened the outside of the boots and carefully wet the inside too, slowly pulling them open as the blood inside dissolved on contact with water. Eddie winced – it smarted – but it was not as painful as just pulling at the boots and breaking the scabs.

Once they had loosened them enough to remove them, Will began to cut away at Eddie's lower trouser leg, using the scissors that came with his first-aid kit. Axel stood close by, collecting strips of bloody fabric as Will handed them to him.

Will felt very grown-up all of a sudden. Like one of the Medical Officers in a field hospital. When both Eddie's legs were free of bloody fabric, he bathed the exposed flesh with water from the bucket until they were almost cleaned of mud and blood. Eddie's calves were pock-marked with little wounds. But Will was sure they wouldn't be fatal. There was a small patch of blood around his thigh as well – which Will would need to look at next.

Will's mother was a nurse and she had taught him well. He felt confident treating other wounded soldiers when the stretcher-bearers and medical orderlies weren't available. Will was proud of his first-aid skills. He'd like to work in a hospital when he got home but he knew he'd never be able to afford the schooling to become a doctor, even if he had the brains, and nursing was a job for lasses.

He used another piece of blanket to dry Eddie's legs off, and then reached for the antiseptic ointment in his kit. 'This will sting a bit,' he told him, but he had passed out again. Will quickly applied the ointment, and used another roll of bandages to dress the wounds.

Axel tapped Will on his arm, causing him to look up. A small circle of middle-aged men stood around them, armed with a motley collection of weapons – pitchfork, various knives, a spade, a single rifle fitted with a bayonet. Will started in fright. He pointed to his uniform. 'English, *Ong-layz, ami,*' . . . He tried to dredge up some more words in his pigeon French, then began to wonder what language these people spoke. They were in Belgium, after all. Was it Flemish? Walloon?

Will looked at their sallow faces. These were men who had spent four years on meagre rations. All of them had cold, hard eyes. The one with the rifle seemed a bit better fed. He had a bowler hat and great black moustache and stood slightly in front of the others. Will supposed he was the leader.

'Allo,' said the man in English. 'We know you are *anglais*. And him –' he pointed with his bayonet. 'What is he?'

'He's American,' said Will. 'His plane was shot down over there.' He pointed to the south-west.

'And he is Boche.' The man pointed his bayonet at Axel. Will said nothing.

At once there was something frightening about these men. 'We need to get help for the flyer,' said Will. 'He's been badly injured.'

The older man would not be deflected. 'Him. What will you do with him?' He pointed again at Axel, who had stayed silent. All of a sudden he looked white with fear.

'He is my prisoner and he is helping me with my wounded ally,' Will announced, trying to sound older and braver than he was.

The man with the black moustache spoke to the others. It was obvious to Will that he was translating, not least because he was mimicking Will's frightened tone. They all laughed when he finished speaking.

'You, Boche,' said the man in German. 'Come here.'

Axel stayed where he was, gripping the side of the wagon as if it would protect him.

'No,' said Will. 'He's been helping us.'

One of them grabbed Axel by the arm and wrenched him away from Will and Eddie. The men began to throw punches and kick him. Will launched himself between Axel and the angry men, trying to push them apart.

He was quickly pulled away, and although they did not hit him, two of the men held him tight enough to prevent him from wriggling free. 'You look after your American friend,' the older man said. 'You leave the Boche to us.'

'No, leave him alone,' shouted Will, realising as the words left his mouth how frightened he sounded.

The man gave him a scornful look. 'We lived with the Boche for four years. Four years we have our crops taken with no recompense, our houses occupy, our wine steal, and they have take hostages and shoot them.'

'But he hasn't had anything to do with that,' shouted Will desperately.

'He is Boche,' said the man plainly.

One of the civilians had come back with a rope, which he was beginning to fashion into a noose. Axel was bloodied and bruised, pinned tightly between two of the burliest men. He was protesting loudly but no one was listening. They were all looking around, wondering where was the best place to rig up a rope and hang him.

At the side of the square was an art-nouveau lamp post with a graceful curving arc close to the top of its metal stand. One of the men pointed and the two holding Axel started to drag him over to this makeshift gallows.

CHAPTER 18

11.50 a.m.

Will opened his mouth to shout. Before he could speak, a shot rang out. Everyone turned to see Eddie Hertz sitting up in the hay wagon, his pistol pointing to the sky.

'That one went into the air,' he announced. 'The next one goes into any one of you who thinks it's a good idea to hang this boy!'

Although few of them actually understood him, his meaning was clear. The two men holding on to Axel let him go and pushed him towards the American.

Will watched tensely, wondering what was going to happen next. The reaction of the crowd seemed mixed. In some there was a resentful defiance, in others there seemed to be shame. Perhaps the American had brought them to their senses. Whatever, they weren't about to kill one of their liberators.

Eddie called to Axel in German. 'Come and stand over here with me. I'm not going to let them kill you.'

The crowd's hostility was rekindled. Pitchforks and shovels were raised again. Eddie realised his mistake. 'Hey, *amis* . . .' he spoke in hesitant French. '*Je suis Americaine. Je parle un peu de alemaine, comprene?*'

Enough of them understood that. There was rapid chatter among them and they backed off again. The atmosphere grew more relaxed. Within a couple of minutes, to Will's complete amazement, some of the men returned with bread and some sort of coffee, which they gave to Eddie and Will – pointedly ignoring Axel.

'Can't say I blame them,' said Eddie to Will in English, as he handed Axel a hunk of bread and offered him his coffee to sip. 'They've been occupied for the last four years. They're bound to be feeling hostile.' His breathing was laboured and his pale face was covered with a thin film of sweat.

'We need to get you some proper medical attention,' Will said to Eddie.

'I think we should sit tight here, until someone from our own side arrives,' said Eddie. The food and drink had lifted his spirits. 'I'm going to be all right, although I'm not sure I'm up to moving right now. I don't think the Germans will be coming back for this . . .' He gestured to the equipment that littered the square. 'I'd say we should tell Axel here to get back to his unit, if he can.'

'But as soon as he's out of our sight the lynch mob will get him,' said Will.

Eddie spoke again in German. 'You stay here, *Kamerad*. You're safe with us.'

Axel showed no sign of wanting to do anything else. Will could see his hands were shaking as he ate the bread Eddie had given him. '*Danke*,' he said.

They waited, anxiously, as a few more people emerged from buildings and gathered in the square. The town was coming back to life. Mostly the civilians kept their distance, but a few eyed Axel with hostility.

'What will happen to me now?' he asked Eddie.

'Wait till our soldiers arrive,' said Eddie. 'I guess you'll be marched to the rear as a prisoner. Sent to a camp, I suppose.'

Axel didn't like the sound of that. If the war really was over, he wanted to get back to his family. But he knew he couldn't risk heading off on his own.

A few minutes later they noticed a khaki-clad figure peering carefully around a building at the edge of the square. The helmet he wore was instantly recognisable. Will shouted loudly, waving his arms. 'Will Franklin, King's Own!'

The man grinned and waved back. Several other soldiers appeared. 'You're safe now,' said Will to Axel, as Eddie translated. 'I'll make sure our lads treat you right.' He ran off to talk to the new arrivals.

A minute later he returned with a British soldier. He was dressed the same as any other only he had a white armband with a red cross on it and carried a hefty bag full of medical equipment. 'This one's got bad shrapnel wounds in the legs,' said Will, as he pointed to Eddie.

The man wiped his eyes with exhaustion and ran a hand along the side of his face, as if trying to keep himself awake. He did not acknowledge Axel at all. 'You don't look too good yourself,' he said to Will. 'Do you want me to look at that head wound?'

Will knew how awful he must look. He was covered in mud and blood, especially around his face. But he also knew it was not serious. 'It's just a bit of bleeding. Looks worse than it is.'

The man examined Eddie, then took Will to one side. 'Find another blanket to keep him warm. And get something to raise his legs up. We need to get him in an ambulance as soon as possible. He's got a bullet in the thigh as well as all those shrapnel wounds. We'll get him cleaned up. Get some blood back into him.

So keep him talking. It's important that he stays conscious.'

Will dashed off at once, and soon returned with two backpacks and another blanket from the pile left by the retreating German troops. The medical orderly had gone.

As Will wrapped the blanket around Eddie, Axel saw another bunch of soldiers arrive in the square. These ones, he quickly noticed, wore the same shoulder badges as Will. The one with a lion under the words 'The King's Own'. He said something and Eddie translated. 'Your comrades have arrived.'

Will looked up to see familiar faces. All at once he felt a surge of excitement and ran over to ask if his brother was with them.

'Haven't seen the sergeant since early this morning,' said one man.

Will's mood abruptly changed. He felt a terrible gnawing anxiety. Jim should have rejoined his unit by now.

'What about Ogden? Hosking?'

The man shook his head. 'Sorry, lad. No sight of any of them.'

Will returned to Eddie and Axel. He remembered the medical orderly's instructions. Keep the wounded man talking. That would keep his mind off Jim.

A young Belgian woman wandered by to peer at the three of them. Eddie started rambling. 'Looks like my girl Janie Holland,' he told Will. 'Same curly brown hair. Not as pretty though.' He laughed. 'Left me for a sailor. From what I heard, he's twiddling his thumbs on a destroyer somewhere south of Iceland. Nice work if you can get it. Nearest they've come to sinking a submarine is spotting a whale!' Eddie let out a long sigh. 'Maybe I should have joined the navy.'

Will heard a familiar voice. It was Lieutenant Richardson. 'Franklin. How did you end up here?' Will explained that they had been ambushed and scattered. 'Have you seen Sergeant Franklin?' he asked eagerly. 'Is he back with the platoon?'

'No sign, nor any of the others on the forest patrol,' said Richardson. 'Still, *nil desperandum*. I'm sure they'll be joining us soon. We're mustering here for a pep talk by the colonel. But I want you to stay here with this injured man. And keep an eye on this Hun lad too. When the ambulance chaps get here, you can take your prisoner to the rear.'

Will nodded. Axel was staring into the distance and looked no threat to anyone. Some colour was coming back to Eddie's cheeks. He would be OK if an ambulance arrived soon. Will racked his brains for things to say, to keep Eddie talking, but it was difficult to think when he didn't know whether his brother was dead or alive.

CHAPTER 19

12.00 noon

The town-hall clock struck out its slow chimes. Axel sat at the side of the square with Will and Eddie. They seemed to have forgotten about him for the moment.

Axel no longer noticed the cold of this chilly November morning. He looked at the leaden sky and the square that was filling up with English soldiers – more King's Own, by the look of their badges – and he felt indifferent to everything. Maybe it was the shock of being nearly blown up and lynched on his first day in combat, or of seeing his comrades killed before his eyes. He felt a great weight of exhaustion, as heavy as the grey sky, pushing down on him. He rested his body against a stone column on the front of the town hall and for a few moments he slept.

He awoke with a start, dreaming about explosions and the horrible sight of that dead soldier in the crater. But he was still alive. In an instant a spring of joy seeped into his soul.

The soldiers in the square seemed strangely muted for a victorious army, almost dazed. While everyone was ignoring him, Axel wondered if he could slip away now, back to his own unit. He supposed they would be somewhere to the east.

But he felt safe where he was, motionless in the corner of the square with Eddie and Will. He was like a sparrow in the forest, perched on a branch beneath the canopy, hidden from circling hawks unless he broke cover into the open sky.

On the far side of the square the soldiers were forming themselves into ranks before the railway station. There were hundreds of them. A sergeant called out and they fell silent. A senior officer, judging by the smartness of his uniform, stood on the steps leading into the station and began to address them all. Axel looked on him with scorn. Here was a man who had been a safe distance away from combat, he supposed, come to the Front, in his shiny boots and immaculate creases and pink, shaved face, for the last hour of the fighting.

As he looked across the square, Axel suddenly remembered where he was. The last few hours had been so extraordinary, so terrible, it had quite escaped him. This was the town he had marched through after they had disembarked from the train. Was it really only nine hours ago he had been here before? It seemed like half a life-time.

As the soldiers continued to gather outside the railway station, he remembered with horror the men he had seen on the roof the previous night. Hadn't they been fixing up explosives? He wanted to call out – warn the British troops. There was no sense in more soldiers being blown to pieces now.

Axel stood up quickly. 'The railway station, it's going to blow up,' he said in German. 'I've just remembered. Last night. When we marched through the town. They were putting explosives on the roof.'

Will stared at him blankly.

Eddie roused himself to translate. 'Axel says the railway station's been wired up – could blow at any minute.'

'We've got to tell them,' said Will. 'Come on!'

The two of them began to walk quickly towards the men lined up in ranks before the station. The colonel was still holding forth – the men were completely silent. Axel could bear it no longer. They were all standing there and could get blown to pieces at any second. He started to call out in German '*Schnell! Rennen Sie weg!*' – Quick! Get out of the way!

They all stopped and looked around. Axel felt terribly

vulnerable. Several of the soldiers raised their rifles and pointed them at him. Will stood in front of him.

'The station,' Will shouted, pointing. 'It's wired with explosives. It might go up at any second. This German soldier is my prisoner. He's just told me.'

'Who is this?' spluttered the colonel. 'What's this Hun blighter doing here? Somebody shoot him and let me get on.'

Fortunately for Axel, no one was prepared to take that remark seriously. A young lieutenant stepped forward and whispered in the colonel's ear. Then the man said, 'But I thought this place had been checked for traps. Rhodes, didn't your men find a bomb in the basement?'

'They did, sir,' said the young lieutenant, 'but if there is another one, they must have missed it. I think we should investigate further.'

Other senior officers began a heated conversation among themselves.

Lieutenant Rhodes grabbed Axel by the arm – not roughly, but like a teacher dealing with an unruly pupil, and certainly firmly enough to make it clear he would not stand for any nonsense. 'What do you know?' he said in passable German.

'Please, sir,' Axel gabbled, 'I was here last night. I

marched through the town. I saw some of our men fixing explosives to the roof.'

'So why are you telling *us*?' asked the officer in a reasonable tone.

'The war is over,' pleaded Axel. 'What is the point of more of you being killed?'

'Stand firm,' bellowed a sergeant. The men snapped to attention in their columns. They were clearly uneasy, but no one was going to break ranks until they were ordered to do so.

'Lieutenant Rhodes,' called the colonel. The young officer went to him and they had a hurried conversation. The colonel spoke in short, angry sentences. Rhodes came back to Axel.

'Whereabouts did you see these explosives?' he asked.

'I couldn't tell exactly,' said Axel. 'It was dark. But I could see them handling wires and sticks of explosive.'

The officer conferred with the colonel again, still holding Axel tightly by the arm. Then he turned to him and said, 'I've been ordered to search the building with you.'

The sergeant bellowed, 'Men, take ten steps backwards.'

The men shuffled awkwardly back. There were a few

uneasy murmurings. 'Silence in the ranks,' shouted the sergeant.

'Rhodes,' called the commander, 'hurry up and take that wretch into the station and see what you can find.'

'Very well, Colonel,' said the lieutenant.

Axel marvelled at his sang froid. 'But it might go up at any second,' he said. 'Please. I don't know where the explosives are – other than somewhere on the roof. Maybe they put them in the gutter.'

The officer instructed Will to return to his post. Then, with one hand gripping Axel's arm, he hurried into the building and up the stairs. For the third or fourth time that day Axel began to feel mortal fear, but this English officer seemed remarkably calm for someone who might be blown to pieces at any moment.

'We found one large cache of explosives in the basement, on a time switch,' he explained, as if he were talking to a colleague. 'Twenty-four-hour fuse. My bomb-disposal boys must have thought that was it.'

'You go first,' said the officer when they came to a closed door in the entrance hall leading to the upper floors. Axel knew he thought the door might be booby-trapped. He refused to go. The officer pulled out his pistol. 'No, after you, I insist,' he said with mock courtesy.

'But if I am killed, how will I be able to help you?' Axel said desperately.

'I'm sure I'll manage,' said the officer.

Axel pushed the door. It opened. Nothing happened.

The next doors they went through were open, and the lieutenant peered through each one, carefully looking for tripwires. But when they reached the door on the second floor leading up to the attic, it too was closed.

'I'll do this one,' said Rhodes. He opened the door a sliver, so the hasp of the lock rested on the door frame. Then he told Axel to step back against the wall. Grabbing a chair that was sitting incongruously in the middle of this empty room, he stood the other side and swung it with all his might against the door, so it flew open. There was an immediate explosion and splinters and fragments, and a large portion of the door, blew out into the room, shattering some of the windows opposite.

The noise from the blast set Axel's ears ringing. He peered into the staircase. It was still there. The charge had blown out rather than down. Rhodes was urging him up the stairs, but Axel could still not hear him. He took a deep breath and suddenly his hearing returned.

Down below in the square Axel could hear a commotion. Out of the window he saw some of the men break ranks. Their rebellion spread like wildfire. The whole group took to their heels and ran to the other end of the square.

'Never mind that. Up to the roof,' Rhodes said. 'There's a skylight up there, we can see down on the eaves easily enough.' Then he said, 'Oh, hang on,' and went over to a shattered window. 'We're both all right,' he called down. Only the sergeant, the colonel and a handful of officers were still there by the railway station. The sergeant was yelling himself hoarse, but the men remained at the far end of the square. The colonel told him to save his breath and dismissed the other officers still there with him.

Axel and the lieutenant hurried up the stairs, hoping the explosion had not made them unsafe. They seemed solid enough. Axel kept wondering if he would be killed at any second by another mine or booby trap left by his comrades.

Like the room downstairs, the attic was empty. Whatever had been kept up here had been taken by the retreating soldiers. 'Quick, climb on my shoulders,' said the lieutenant. 'Have a look through that skylight. See what you can see.'

Rhodes braced himself against the wall and cupped his hands so Axel could climb up. It was an awkward business, but he managed to haul himself up and was just tall enough to be able to peer out of the skylight.

'I can't see anything,' said Axel. He was beginning to sweat, despite the cold. If the building went up, they would be blown apart or buried in rubble. He had survived the war. He didn't want to die now. 'Down you come,' said the lieutenant, and Axel leaped down, landing on the bare wooden floorboards with a loud thump.

Rhodes accepted his observation. 'There must be something,' he said. He darted over to the chimney. 'Maybe it's up *here*.' He took a small pocket torch from his jacket and pointed it up the chimney shaft.

'A-ha! So there you are,' he said to himself, and Axel froze. He recognised that tone, even if he didn't understand the words. He called Axel over, and handed him his torch. 'Look at that – taped just inside the chimney breast. Standard detonation device. Acid eating through a wire, I imagine. When did you see your fellows up on the roof?'

Axel racked his brains. 'About three in the morning, I think.'

'These things usually go off after one or two hours, sometimes six or nine.' He looked at his watch, then said decisively, 'Let's go. It could go off any second.' Axel didn't need to be told twice. He ran down the stairs three at a time, the lieutenant right behind him.

Axel burst out of the main entrance to find the colonel and the sergeant standing right outside by the awning. The rest of the soldiers were still at the far side of the square, waiting to see what would happen.

Axel wondered if the colonel felt he had to stay where he had commanded his men to stand. Maybe he was braver than Axel had first thought. Maybe he felt he had to share the danger with this junior officer he had sent into the building. Axel also admired the loyalty of the Sergeant.

Rhodes had run down the stairs too, but as he got to the entrance hall Axel could see he had stopped for a moment to catch his breath. He sauntered out, trying to look as unhurried and unflustered as possible.

'There is a large explosive charge in the chimney, sir,' he said as he saluted.

'Very well, Rhodes, well done. A regrettable lapse, though, on behalf of your search team. Surely they should have looked in the attic as well as the basement.'

'Indeed, sir. I shall speak to them.'

'And what do you suggest we do now?'

'I think we need to retire a safe distance immediately,

sir,' said Rhodes. 'The charge was set around nine hours ago. I wouldn't recommend removing it.'

'Very well, Lieutenant,' said the colonel, and both of them walked in silence, at a deliberately leisurely pace, towards the men on the other side of the square. The colonel, especially, was not going to hurry.

Axel's instincts told him to run though. Some of the men gathered on the far side of the square laughed at him, but some of them cheered too and clapped him on the back when he passed through them.

He sought out Will and Eddie, who were where he had left them at the corner and away from the other soldiers. Will greeted him with a great beaming smile, a hand-shake and a heartfelt 'Thank you!'

The colonel was composing a speech in his head, one that would save face, telling his men he would overlook their disobedience on this great historical occasion. Inside the chimney the acid finally ate through the thin steel wire in the filling cap. A strong spring immediately drove a striker bolt into the detonator, which ignited six sticks of high explosives.

The blast shook the entire town, shattering window-panes and blowing open doors all around the square. The roof of the station collapsed in a great cloud and brought down the top two storeys with it. When the smoke cleared, Lieutenant Rhodes was still standing, although he looked dazed. The colonel was lying on the cobbled square.

Some of the men rushed over to help. Rhodes was filthy with brick dust, but he was all right. The colonel was coughing and trying to stand unaided, his dignity in tatters.

CHAPTER 20

1.00 p.m.

Rhodes limped over to Axel, who was standing with Will, staring at the great cloud of smoke and dust rising from the railway station.

'Top hole,' he said to him, speaking incomprehensible English. 'Rotten luck if we'd copped it, eh!' Then he held out his hand to shake. 'Lieutenant Rhodes. No hard feelings,' he said with a smile.

He turned to Will. 'I think we ought to let this fellow go.'

Speaking to Axel in German he said, 'We're supposed to consider you a prisoner of war, but I think it would be better if you headed off east to the German lines – catch up with your unit. They can't be far. If we hold on to you, you'll probably have to go to a prison camp in England and it'll be months before you get home. If you go now, you might be back with your family before the week's out.'

'Thank you,' said Axel. 'I would like to do that. But I'm worried about the townspeople here. They tried to kill me before you arrived.'

'You wait here a second,' said Rhodes. 'I'll sort that out. Oh, and you'll need something to eat and drink.'

He walked down the street to a British supply trailer and spoke to the soldier who was guarding it. Then he returned with a ration pack and a water bottle. 'That'll keep you going, lad. You can go now.'

Axel was moved almost to tears. 'And hang on,' said Rhodes, 'I'm coming with you. I'll take you to the edge of town in case anyone else thinks it's a bright idea to detain you.'

Axel turned to Will and Eddie and gave them a stiff salute. '*Danke, dass Sie mir das Leben gerettet haben,*' he said. '*Ich wünsche Ihnen Glück!*' Thank you for saving my life. I wish you well.

Axel could see Will wasn't sure he wanted to salute a German, so he put out his hand again. 'Thank you for what you did,' Will said. 'I wish we could have been friends.' Axel didn't understand the words, but he saw a tear in his eye.

The town was small, and Axel was soon on the outskirts. He liked having Rhodes with him, although neither could think of anything to say to the other.

The events of the day had been too momentous for pleasantries.

Rhodes looked around. There was no one about. The road ahead was deserted.

'Can't see any of the locals. I think you'll be safe. Go quickly. And here, have a bar of chocolate too,' he said, and bid Axel farewell.

Axel saluted again and Rhodes returned his salute with a smile. Then he turned and hurried back to his unit.

Axel continued down the road out of town. The further he got, the safer he felt. The chocolate bar Rhodes had given him felt like a bar of gold in his hand. This bar was not army issue, its packaging was too gaudy – five paintings of the face of a young boy with five different expressions – from worried to delighted. It seemed odd, after such horror and deprivation – to see something so jaunty, so frivolous.

Axel tore off the paper and the silver foil and broke a chunk off. He savoured the moment, the bittersweet aroma, the lovely crumbly feel of the stuff, melting slightly in his filthy hand. He had stopped worrying about washing his hands a week into basic training. He popped it into his mouth and as it dissolved on his tongue he was transported home to Wansdorf and the last time he had eaten chocolate. He had been twelve then – still singing in the church choir. His mother had given him the chocolate as a reward. Axel had sung his first solo at the Sunday Eucharist, the Bach cantata *Ich Habe Genug*, and the whole family had come to listen. He had never felt more proud in his life. Even poor Otto, his older brother, had come.

He imagined his sister's face as he returned to the village. He could picture how pleased Gretl would be to see him. Now the war was over, maybe he could find work playing the piano in the halls and taverns in Berlin. And maybe, when Gretl was a little older, she could sing alongside him.

His pace picked up. He felt a vigour he had not felt for weeks – he was going home.

The sun poked out for a brief moment, and Axel felt its warmth on his face. He swallowed the smooth chocolate, thinking he had never tasted anything quite so delicious. He broke another piece and let it melt on his tongue, stopping to savour the moment. He decided then and there he was going to eat the whole bar. When he got back to the German lines, he certainly wasn't going to share this with strangers!

On the top floor of his house on the edge of the town, Georges de Winne squinted through the sights of his rifle. When the Germans went last night, he had finally plucked up the courage to steal a few rounds of ammunition from a pack they had left in the square. The German boy was at the edge of his range, he reckoned, but the sudden burst of sunlight made it easier to draw a bead on him. And, for the moment, he was standing still. Perfect. He wasn't going to let that Boche go; he didn't care what age he was. Four years they'd lived in his house and eaten his food. He felt a mounting rage – one that he had nursed and nurtured over the long years of occupation. De Winne held his breath and his finger tightened around the trigger.

When Axel vanished from sight, Will turned his attention again to Eddie. He was asleep or unconscious. Where was the ambulance? Will tried to shake him awake. Failing to rouse him, he ran off to look for medical orderlies. It had been over half an hour since the first orderly had seen them.

Will couldn't find anyone from the Medical Corps so he decided to look for an ambulance himself, searching each side street for a dirty brown vehicle with a red cross on the side. After three minutes, he saw one in the distance, close to the road that led past the railway station, and ran over to talk to the driver. There were orderlies inside, and he could even see the white headscarf of a nurse. 'We have a pilot, badly injured, on the far side of the square,' he said, trying not to sound too upset. 'He needs attention. I can't rouse him.'

The driver patted a hand on his and told him to return to the injured man. The road ahead was blocked with fallen debris, he explained. They would find another route and come to attend to this man as soon as possible. Will was to wave and identify his position as soon as the ambulance found a way into the square.

Will rushed back, desperately hoping he might find Jim on the way. Eddie was still unconscious but his breathing was regular. And his colour looked better than it had been. Maybe he was just exhausted. Will put a hand on his shoulder. 'They're coming, Eddie,' he said. 'You hold on a little longer.'

A minute or two later he heard the judder of an internal combustion engine and saw the nose of the ambulance peep from a nearby side street. Will cheered with relief and stood up to wave them over.

At that moment a loud blast ripped through the square close to where he was standing. In an instant Will felt the heat of the explosion burn his face, then a sharp stab – like the blade of a knife at the top of his forehead – then nothing.

*　　*　　*

195

Over on the far side of town, Georges de Winne is startled by the sudden blast. The bullet he releases merely grazes the side of Axel's head.

Axel falls to the ground. There is a sharp pain just above his ear, but he quickly realises he has not been seriously injured. Gathering his thoughts, he runs as fast as he can. Bullets punch the ground around him, but de Winne has run out of ammunition by the time Axel finds shelter in a nearby copse. Blood is pouring down the side of his head. But it is only a flesh wound. In the distance he can see the smoking chimney of a *Gulaschkanone*. He runs forward, breathlessly calling out to the soldiers as he approaches.

Back in the square the ambulance crew tumble from their vehicle, thinking an artillery barrage is falling on the town. They crouch close to the wall, awaiting further destruction.

'Which bloody idiot is still firing shells?' asks the driver. 'The war's supposed to be over.'

'Maybe it was one of ours with a delayed-action fuse?' says a stretcher-bearer. 'There was an assault planned here for this morning.' He sighs. 'Maybe they sent it over the night before.'

There are no more explosions so they peer around the corner. Close by, they see the facade of one of the buildings overlooking the square has fallen in on itself. The blast has overturned a hay cart and two bodies are lying lifeless on the ground.

The nurse quickly gathers her medical kit. Most of the time she works in the field hospitals, but sometimes she goes out behind the front line, acting as a translator for the British.

'I'll go,' she volunteers. 'You see who else might have been caught in the blast.'

She walks towards the two prone bodies with her usual detachment. She heard the morning's news, of course, but like so many others she feels indifference, perhaps a mild relief that it is over. It is too late for her fiancé, Auguste, and her brother Julien. But as she approaches she feels a small stab of pity for these two before her. Caught on the last morning. The fortunes of war.

Both of them are still. There is blood, but nothing missing or torn open. Nothing too grotesque. One wears a leather flying helmet, the other is the British boy they spoke to a few minutes ago.

She goes to the airman first. As she kneels down, she can see he is breathing, just, but she instinctively knows he isn't long for the world. He is 'expectant' – the field-hospital triage category for beyond help.

The British boy lies motionless and is covered with mud and dried blood. He is as limp as a rag doll and there is no pulse. There is a fresh wound on his forehead but otherwise he seems unmarked by the blast. She has seen it many times. Artillery shells and bombs have unpredictable effects on their victims. Some would be turned almost inside out with the force of an explosion. Others would seem asleep, with slight or no visible wounds – only the terrible stillness of the dead.

She turns again to look at the pale, bloodied face of the airman and recognition dawns. With a start she sees the edge of her scarf poking just above the neckline of his leather jacket. It is that pilot she often sees at the American airbase. She likes him, he is sweet, although he does remind her of a frisky puppy, always buying her drinks and trying to talk to her. All that joie de vivre snuffed out like a candle. What a terrible waste. He had such an appetite for life. What was his name? Eddie. She had seen him just last night. It had been a wild evening, with too much wine, and everyone singing songs around the piano. When he'd asked for her scarf as a good-luck charm, she didn't want to hurt his feelings. After all, it had only cost her fifty centimes in a little junk shop in Paris.

She touches his face with her hand and leans closer

to talk to him. 'Hello, Eddie. It's me, Céline. Can you hear me?'

The sound seeps through to Eddie's fading consciousness, and something in his dying mind stirs. They are sitting on the grass at the Tuileries Garden, close to the Louvre. She is resting her head on his shoulder and caressing his face. The sunlight is brighter than he could ever imagine and he is so happy he feels like he is floating in the air.

Two other men from the ambulance crew come over carrying a stretcher apiece. They place them on the ground and lift Will Franklin and Eddie Hertz on to them. One of the stretcher men goes over to the ambulance to fetch a couple of blankets.

'I'll stay with this one for a moment, if you don't mind,' says Céline, still crouching by the airman. And she stays with him until she is sure his breathing has ceased. She pulls the blanket over his head. The young British soldier lying close by with blood all over his face hasn't moved a jot. She shakes her head and looks around for other injured men who might need her attention.

A few minutes later an orderly approaches the two lifeless bodies. 'Have you done their tags?' he asks a man with Red Cross armbands.

'Not yet,' he replies.

The soldier pulls back the blankets and briskly snaps off one of the two identity tags Will and Eddie both wear around their neck. He looks at Will's. 'Thought so,' he says to himself. 'That's Sergeant Franklin's brother. I wouldn't like to be the one to tell him.'

He turns to his companion and says, 'We'll come back for these two later,' and walks away.

On the far side of the town square Sergeant Jim Franklin has caught up with his platoon. When the shooting in the forest started again, all of them, even he, just snapped and fled like frightened starlings. They had scattered out of pure terror, each one expecting that bullet in the brain, each one operating on pure survival instinct.

By the time Sergeant Franklin came to his senses, only Ogden was still there with him. Hosking soon caught up with them. Will had vanished.

'Not a word,' Franklin had warned them. 'Not a word of this to a soul.'

They walked back to their previous position and some artillery men told them their unit had gone into Saint-Libert. And had they heard the news? The war was over. Jim Franklin was too tired to be happy and too upset about the men he had just lost. And he was too worried about his brother.

Now an anxious man runs up to speak to him and points. Jim walks towards the two stretchers he can see placed on the cobbled ground at the far end of the square. The railway station is still billowing smoke, but he barely notices. Everything seems to be taking place in a dream. His feet move forward on the solid ground but Franklin feels like he is wading through a morass of deep, sucking mud. His throat is tight, his chest heavy; he curses himself for having lost Will in the woods.

Jim approaches his brother's shroud, wondering how on earth he is going to explain all this to his mother. He can picture her on the doorstep, getting that black-bordered telegram.

Choking back the tears that rise like floodwater, he pushes away the blanket. The blank eyes of Eddie Hertz stare back at him. Jim sees at once this man is a pilot and pulls the blanket back over his face.

His eyes alight on the other covered stretcher, but he is too overcome to look. He thinks of Will's face – the lad had barely started shaving – and he begins to cry great gasping sobs. He sits on the cobble square and it all comes flooding out. For the first time ever he doesn't care if the men see him. The sodding war is over now. They can think what they bloody well like.

Far in the distance, Will hears a strange wailing sound. His ears are still ringing, and he has a terrible pain in his head. There is a stifling, musty smell in his nose and an itchy, scratchy feeling on his face. He wonders if he is dead, but his rational mind dismisses the idea. He remembers a great flash and then nothing. He seems to be far, far underwater, but he is slowly coming to the surface.

Jim pulls back the blanket from his brother's face just as his eyes flicker open.

FACT AND FICTION

Eleven Eleven is structured around the final day of the Great War. Altogether, close to three thousand soldiers on both sides died on that final morning. Most fatalities occurred along the American sections of the front line as many American soldiers were ordered to fight to the last minute. An unlucky few on both sides were killed after eleven o'clock, in misunderstandings, and from stray artillery fire and unexploded shells.

In Chapter 6 the signing of the Armistice on Marshal Foch's private train in Compiègne Forest is based on eyewitness accounts, although the narrator of this chapter, Captain Atherley, is fictitious.

All other characters, and what happens to them in the novel, are fictitious, although their age reflects the youth of many participants in the war. The Belgian town of St Libert, close to Mons and the French border, does not exist. Aulnois and Prouvy do, but were not affected by the events in the book.

William Franklin, Axel Meyer and Eddie Hertz are based on no real individuals, and the fighting units they belong to are either fictitious or took part in other actions on that day.

Because the story is set at the very end of the Great War, *Eleven Eleven* does not depict the suffering of soldiers on all sides caught up in the interminable trench warfare of 1914–1918. Have a look at *L'enfer* by Georges Leroux on Google Images to get a glimpse into why this conflict still haunts us a hundred years later.

ACKNOWLEDGEMENTS

A big thank you to Ele Fountain and Isabel Ford, my two invaluable editors at Bloomsbury, Dilys Dowswell, who read and commented on all my first drafts, and Neil Offley who helped me fulfil a long-held ambition to visit some of the battlefields and memorials of the Western Front. Christian Staufenbiel kindly gave his time to advise on the German words I've used.

And thanks, as ever, to my agent, Charlie Viney, for his tireless support, and Jenny and Josie Dowswell for looking after me.

PICK UP THE NEXT
INCREDIBLE THRILLER FROM
PAUL DOWSWELL . . .

AUSLÄNDER

'DOWSWELL SHOWS US A SIDE OF
NAZI GERMANY RARELY SEEN . . .
A HEART-STOPPING READ'

SUNDAY TELEGRAPH

TURN OVER TO READ CHAPTER 1

CHAPTER 1

Warsaw
August 2, 1941

Piotr Bruck shivered in the cold as he waited with twenty or
so other naked boys in the long draughty corridor. He
carried his clothes in an untidy bundle and hugged them
close to his chest to try to keep warm. The late summer day
was overcast and the rain had not let up since daybreak. He
could see the goose pimples on the scrawny shoulder of the
boy in front. That boy was shivering too, maybe from cold,
maybe from fear. Two men in starched white coats sat at a
table at the front of the line. They were giving each boy a
cursory examination with strange-looking instruments.
Some boys were sent to the room at the left of the table.
Others were curtly dismissed to the room at the right.

Piotr and the other boys had been ordered to be silent
and not look around. He willed his eyes to stay firmly
fixed forward. So strong was Piotr's fear, he felt almost
detached from his body. Every movement he made

seemed unnatural, forced. The only thing keeping him in the here and now was a desperate ache in his bladder. Piotr knew there was no point asking for permission to use the lavatory. When the soldiers had descended on the orphanage to hustle the boys from their beds and into a waiting van, he had asked to go. But he got a sharp cuff round the ear for talking out of turn.

The soldiers had first come to the orphanage two weeks ago. They had been back several times since. Sometimes they took boys, sometimes girls. Some of the boys in Piotr's overcrowded dormitory had been glad to see them go: 'More food for us, more room too, what's the problem?' said one. Only a few of the children came back. Those willing to tell what had happened had muttered something about being photographed and measured.

Now, just ahead in the corridor, Piotr could see several soldiers in black uniforms. The sort with lightning insignia on the collars. Some had dogs – fierce Alsatians who strained restlessly at their chain leashes. He had seen men like this before. They had come to his village during the fighting. He had seen first-hand what they were capable of.

There was another man watching them. He wore the same lightning insignia as the soldiers, but his was bold and large on the breast pocket of his white coat. He stood close to Piotr, tall and commanding, arms held behind his back, overseeing this mysterious procedure. When he turned around, Piotr noticed he carried a short leather riding whip. The man's dark hair flopped lankly over the top of his head, but it was shaved at the sides, in the German style, a good seven or eight centimetres above the ears.

Observing the boys through black-rimmed spectacles he would nod or shake his head as his eyes passed along the line. Most of the boys, Piotr noticed, were blond like him, although a few had darker hair.

The man had the self-assured air of a doctor, but what he reminded Piotr of most was a farmer, examining his pigs and wondering which would fetch the best price at the village market. He caught Piotr staring and tutted impatiently through tight, thin lips, signalling for him to look to the front with a brisk, semicircular motion of his index finger.

Now Piotr was only three rows from the table, and could hear snippets of the conversation between the two men there. 'Why was this one brought in?' Then louder to the boy before him. 'To the right, quick, before you feel my boot up your arse.'

Piotr edged forward. He could see the room to the right led directly to another corridor and an open door that led outside. No wonder there was such a draught. Beyond was a covered wagon where he glimpsed sullen young faces and guards with bayonets on their rifles. He felt another sharp slap to the back of his head. 'Eyes forward!' yelled a soldier. Piotr thought he was going to wet himself, he was so terrified.

On the table was a large box file. Stencilled on it in bold black letters were the words:

RACE AND SETTLEMENT MAIN OFFICE

Now Piotr was at the front of the queue praying hard not to be sent to the room on the right. One of the men in the starched white coats was looking directly at him. He smiled and turned to his companion who was reaching for a strange device that reminded Piotr of a pair of spindly pincers. There were several of these on the table. They looked like sinister medical instruments, but their purpose was not to extend or hold open human orifices or surgical incisions. These pincers had centimetre measurements indented along their polished steel edges.

'We hardly need to bother,' he said to his companion. 'He looks just like that boy in the Hitler-Jugend poster.'

They set the pincers either side of his ears, taking swift measurements of his face. The man indicated he should go to the room on the left with a smile. Piotr scurried in. There, other boys were dressed and waiting. As his fear subsided, he felt foolish standing there naked, clutching his clothes. There were no soldiers here, just two nurses, one stout and maternal, the other young and petite. Piotr blushed crimson. He saw a door marked Herren and dashed inside.

The ache in his bladder gone, Piotr felt light-headed with relief. They had not sent him to the room on the right and the covered wagon. He was here with the nurses. There was a table with biscuits, and tumblers and a jug of water. He found a spot over by the window and hurriedly dressed. He had arrived at the orphanage with only the clothes he stood up in and these were a second set they had given him. He sometimes wondered who his grubby pullover had belonged to and hoped its previous owner had grown out of it rather than died.

Piotr looked around at the other boys here with him. He recognised several faces but there was no one here he would call a friend.

Outside in the corridor he heard the scrape of wood on polished floor. The table was being folded away. The selection was over. The last few boys quickly dressed as the older nurse clapped her hands to call everyone to attention.

'Children,' she said in a rasping German accent, stumbling clumsily round the Polish words. 'Very important gentleman here to talk. Who speak German?'

No one came forward.

'Come now,' she smiled. 'Do not be shy.'

Piotr could sense that this woman meant him no harm. He stepped forward, and addressed her in fluent German.

'Well, you are a clever one,' she replied in German, putting a chubby arm around his shoulder. 'Where did you learn to speak like that?'

'My parents, miss,' said Piotr. 'They both speak –' Then he stopped and his voice faltered. 'They both spoke German.'

The nurse hugged him harder as he fought back tears. No one had treated him this kindly at the orphanage.

'Now who are you, mein Junge?' she said. Between sobs he blurted out his name.

'Pull yourself together, young Piotr,' she whispered in German. 'The Doktor is not the most patient fellow.'

The tall, dark-haired man Piotr had seen earlier strolled into the room. He stood close to the nurse and asked her which of the boys spoke German. 'Just give me a moment with this one,' she said. She turned back to Piotr and said gently, 'Now dry those eyes. I want you to tell these children what the Doktor says.'

She pinched his cheek and Piotr stood nervously at the front of the room, waiting for the man to begin talking.

He spoke loudly, in short, clear sentences, allowing Piotr time to translate.

'My name is Doktor Fischer . . . I have something very special to tell you . . . You boys have been chosen as candidates . . . for the honour of being reclaimed by the German National Community . . . You will undergo further examinations . . . to establish your racial value . . . and whether or not you are worthy of such an honour . . . Some of you will fail and be sent back to your own people.'

He paused, looking them over like a stern schoolteacher.

'Those of you who are judged to be Volksdeutsche – of German blood – will be taken to the Fatherland . . . and found good German homes and German families.'

Piotr felt a glimmer of excitement, but as the other boys listened their eyes grew wide with shock. The room fell silent. Doktor Fischer turned on his heels and was gone. Then there was uproar – crying and angry shouting. Immediately, the Doktor sprang back into the room and cracked his whip against the door frame. Two soldiers stood behind him.

'How dare you react with such ingratitude. You will assist my staff in this process,' he yelled and the noise subsided instantly. 'And you will not want to be one of those left behind.'

Piotr shouted out these final remarks in Polish. He was too preoccupied trying to translate this stream of words to notice an angry boy walking purposefully towards him. The boy punched him hard on the side of the head and knocked him to the floor. 'Traitor,' he spat, as he was dragged away by a soldier.

SEKTION 20

'A GREAT THRILLER WITH A POIGNANT
HISTORICAL BACKGROUND . . . TERRIFIC'
BOOKSELLER

Alex lives in East Berlin. The Cold War is raging and
he and his family are forbidden to leave. But the longer
he stays, the more danger he is in. Alex is no longer
pretending to be a model East German, and the Stasi
have noticed. They are watching him.
One false move will bring East and West together in a
terrifying stand-off which will change everything for
Alex and his family . . . for ever.